JOHNNY BOO

AND THE MEAN LITTLE BOY

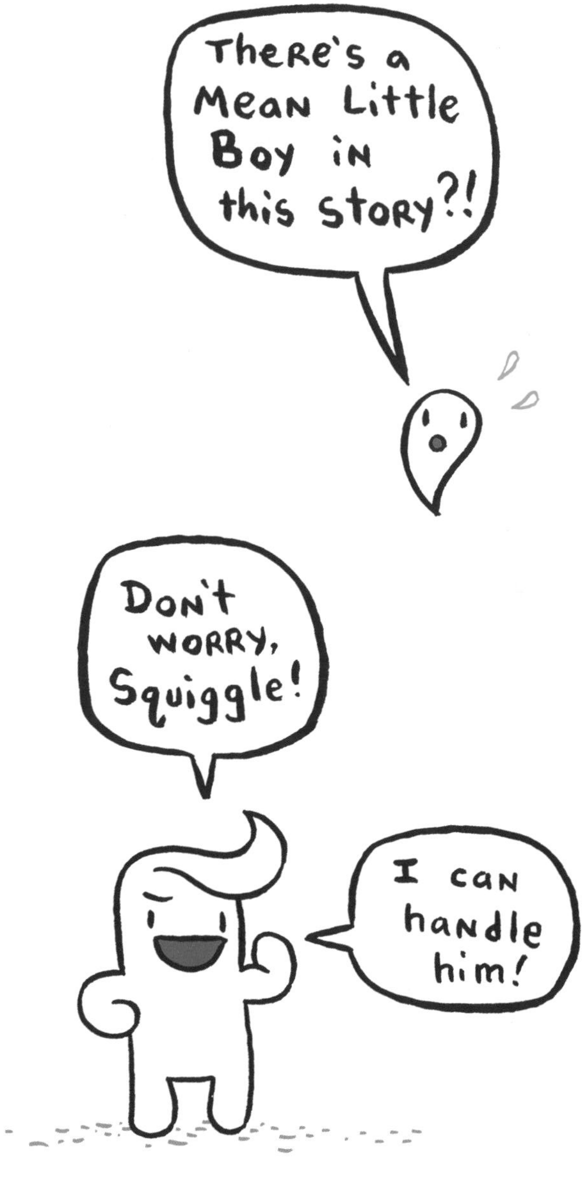
There's a Mean Little Boy in this story?!
Don't worry, Squiggle!
I can handle him!

Other books by
James Kochalka

Johnny Boo: The Best Little Ghost in the World
Johnny Boo: Twinkle Power
Johnny Boo & the Happy Apples
Dragon Puncher
Pinky & Stinky
Monkey Vs. Robot
Monkey Vs. Robot and the Crystal of Power
Peanutbutter & Jeremy's Best Book Ever
Squirrelly Gray

Johnny Boo and the Mean Little Boy
© 2010 James Kochalka.

Editor-in-Chief: Chris Staros.

ISBN: 978-1-60309-059-9

1. Children's Books
2. Ghosts
3. Graphic Novels

Published by Top Shelf Productions, an imprint of IDW
Publishing, a division of Idea and Design Works, LLC.
Offices: Top Shelf Productions, c/o Idea & Design Works,
LLC, 2765 Truxtun Road, San Diego, CA 92106. Top Shelf
Productions®, the Top Shelf logo, Idea and Design
Works®, and the IDW logo are registered trademarks
of Idea and Design Works, LLC. All Rights Reserved.
With the exception of small excerpts of artwork used
for review purposes, none of the contents of this
publication may be reprinted without the permission of
IDW Publishing. IDW Publishing does not read or accept
unsolicited submissions of ideas, stories, or artwork.
Visit our online catalog at www.topshelfcomix.com.
Third Printing, March 2020. Printed in Korea.

CHAPTER ONE:

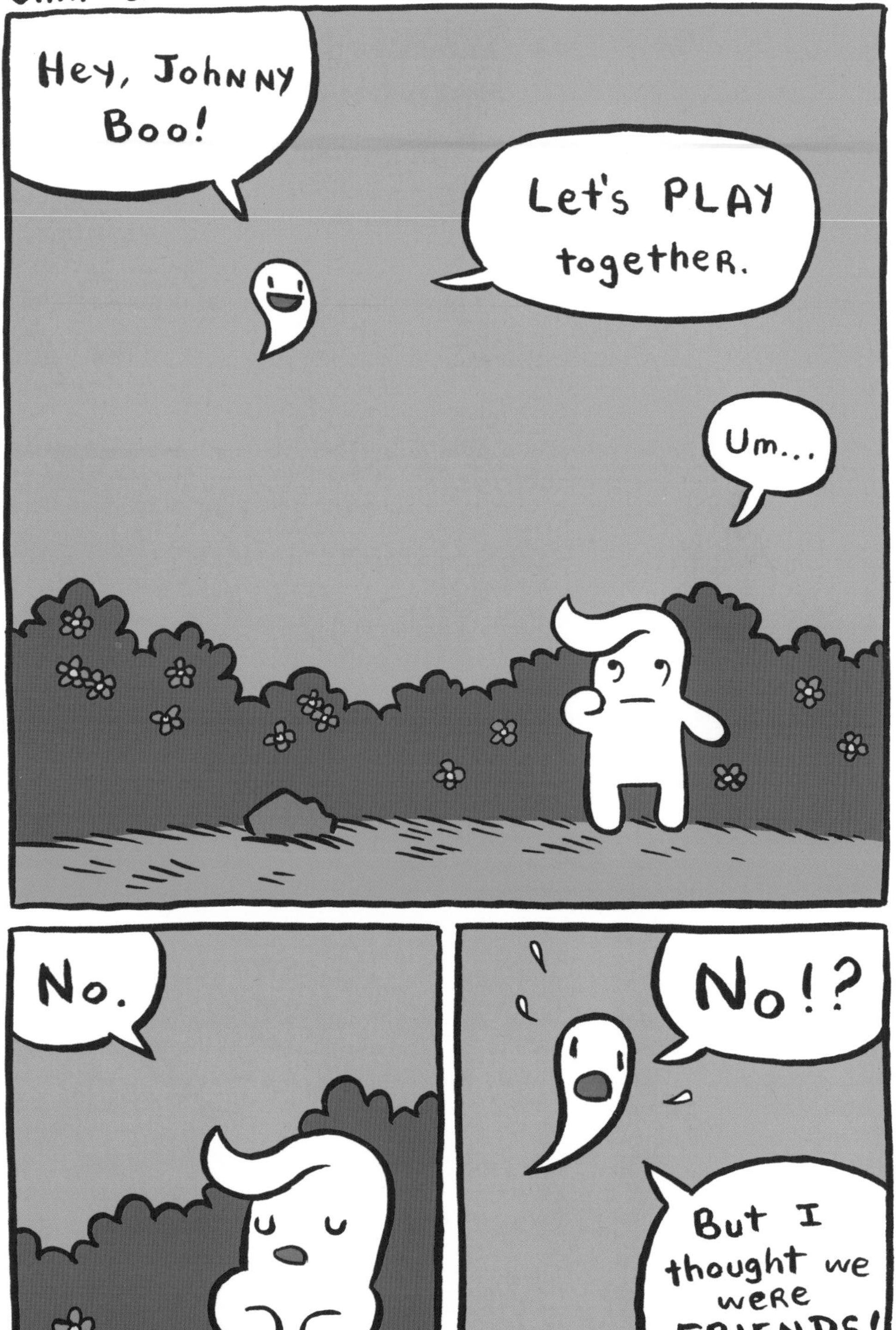
Hey, Johnny Boo!
Let's PLAY together.
Um...
No.
No!?
But I thought we were FRIENDS!

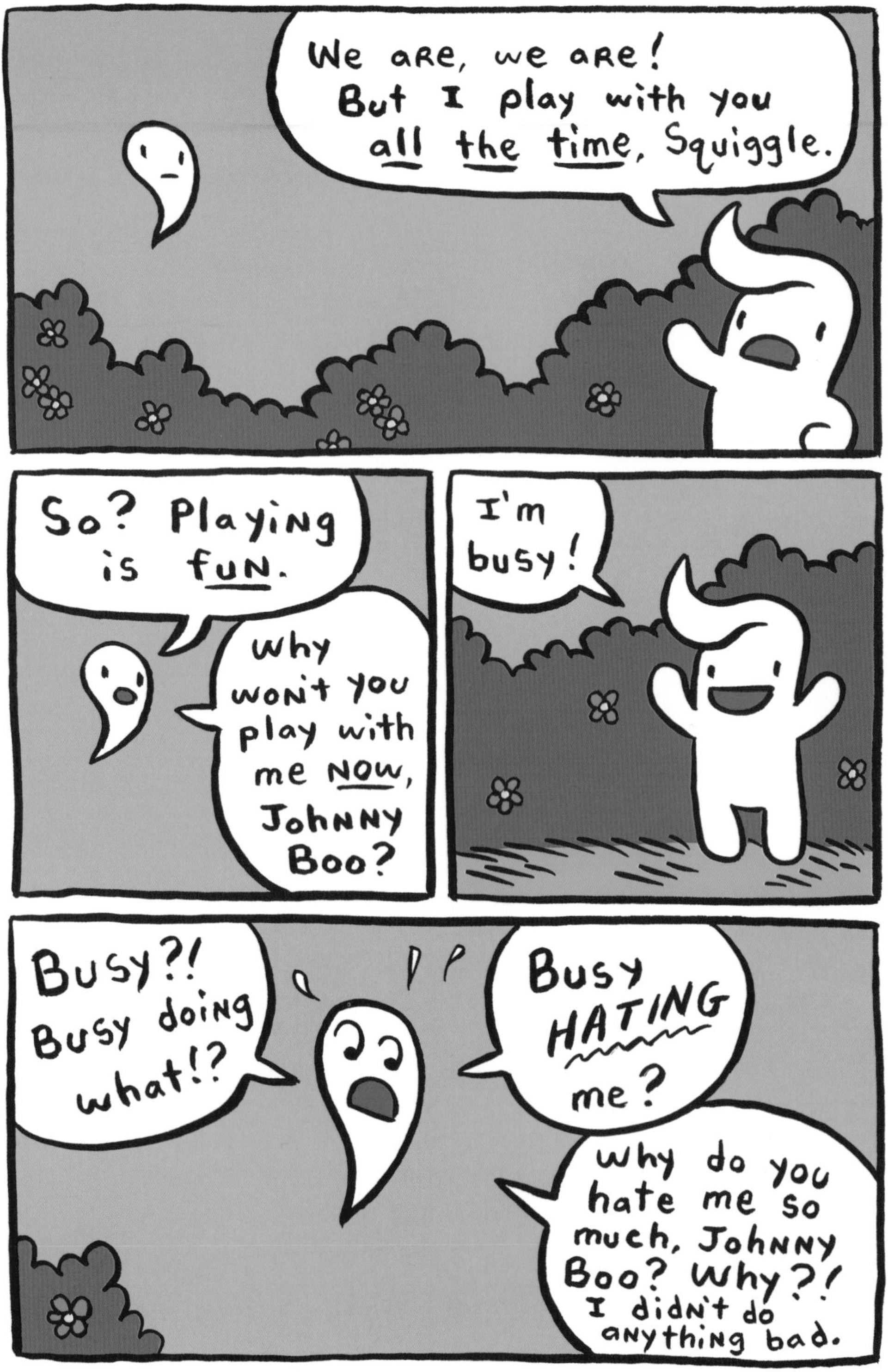

We are, we are! But I play with you all the time, Squiggle.
So? Playing is fun.
Why won't you play with me NOW, Johnny Boo?
I'm busy!
Busy?! Busy doing what!?
Busy HATING me?
Why do you hate me so much, Johnny Boo? Why?! I didn't do anything bad.

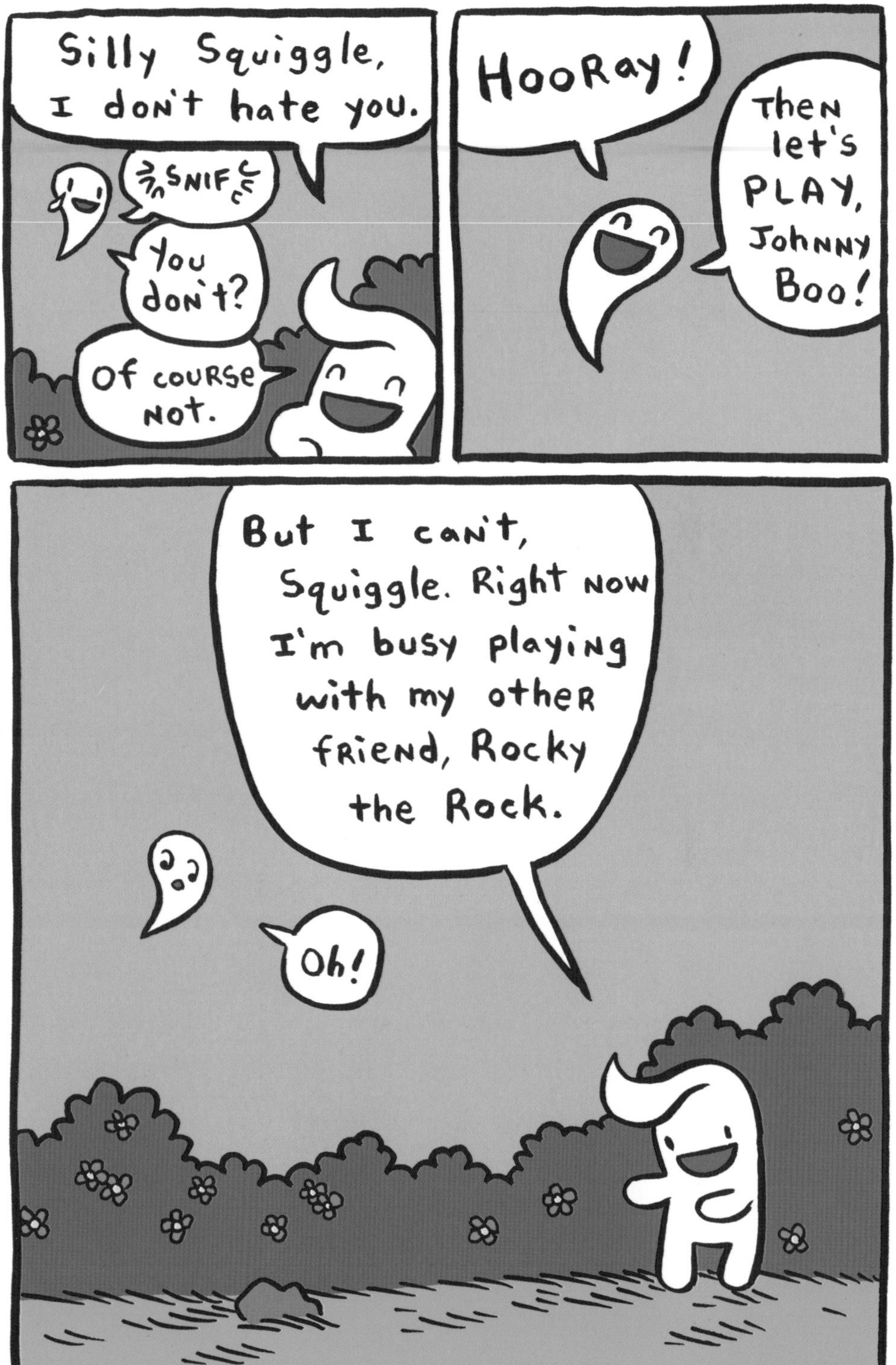
Silly Squiggle, I don't hate you.
SNIF
You don't?
Of course not.
HOORAY!
Then let's PLAY, Johnny Boo!
But I can't, Squiggle. Right now I'm busy playing with my other friend, Rocky the Rock.
Oh!

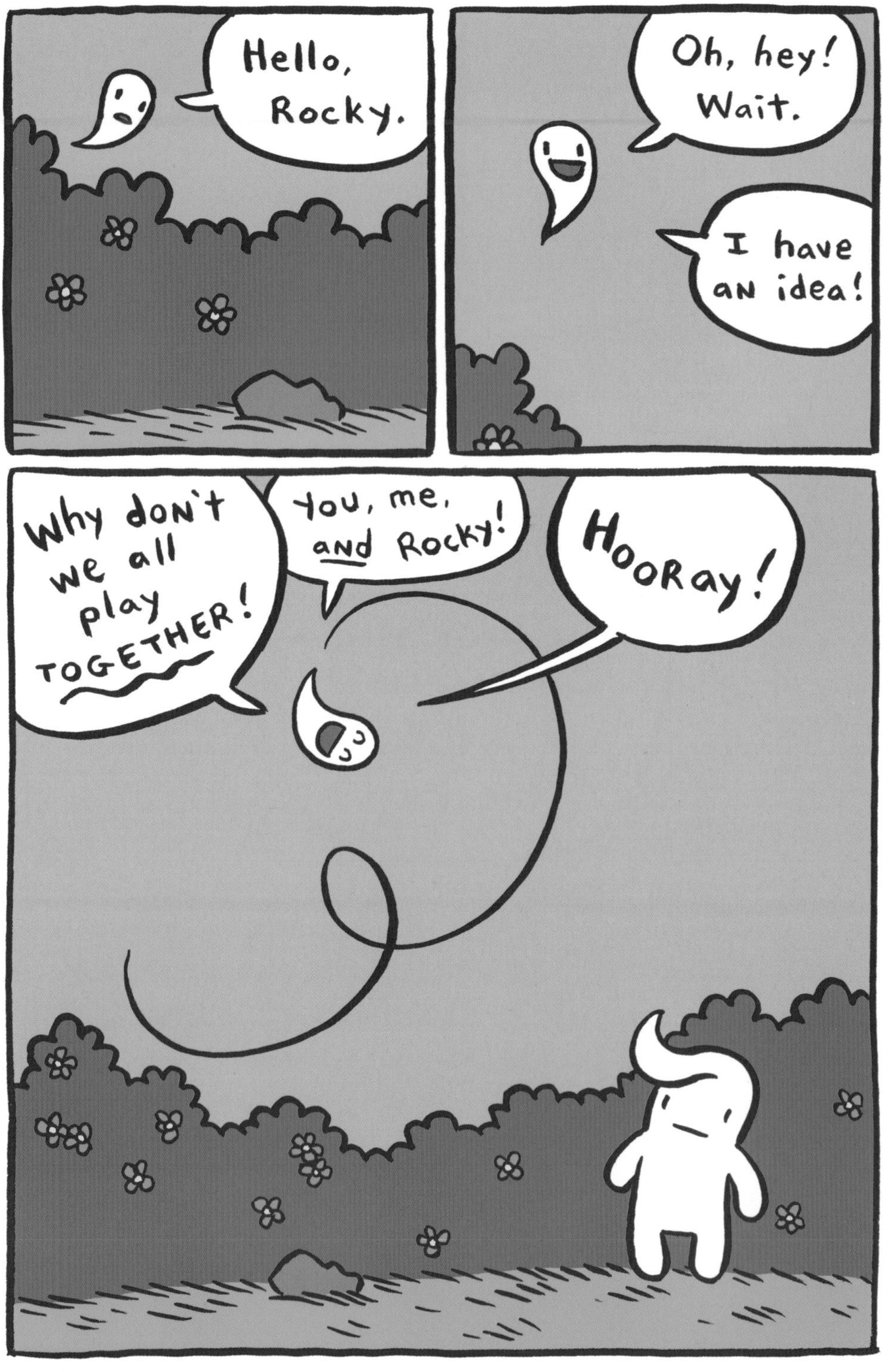
Hello, Rocky.
Oh, hey! Wait.
I have an idea!
Why don't we all play TOGETHER!
You, me, and Rocky!
HOORay!

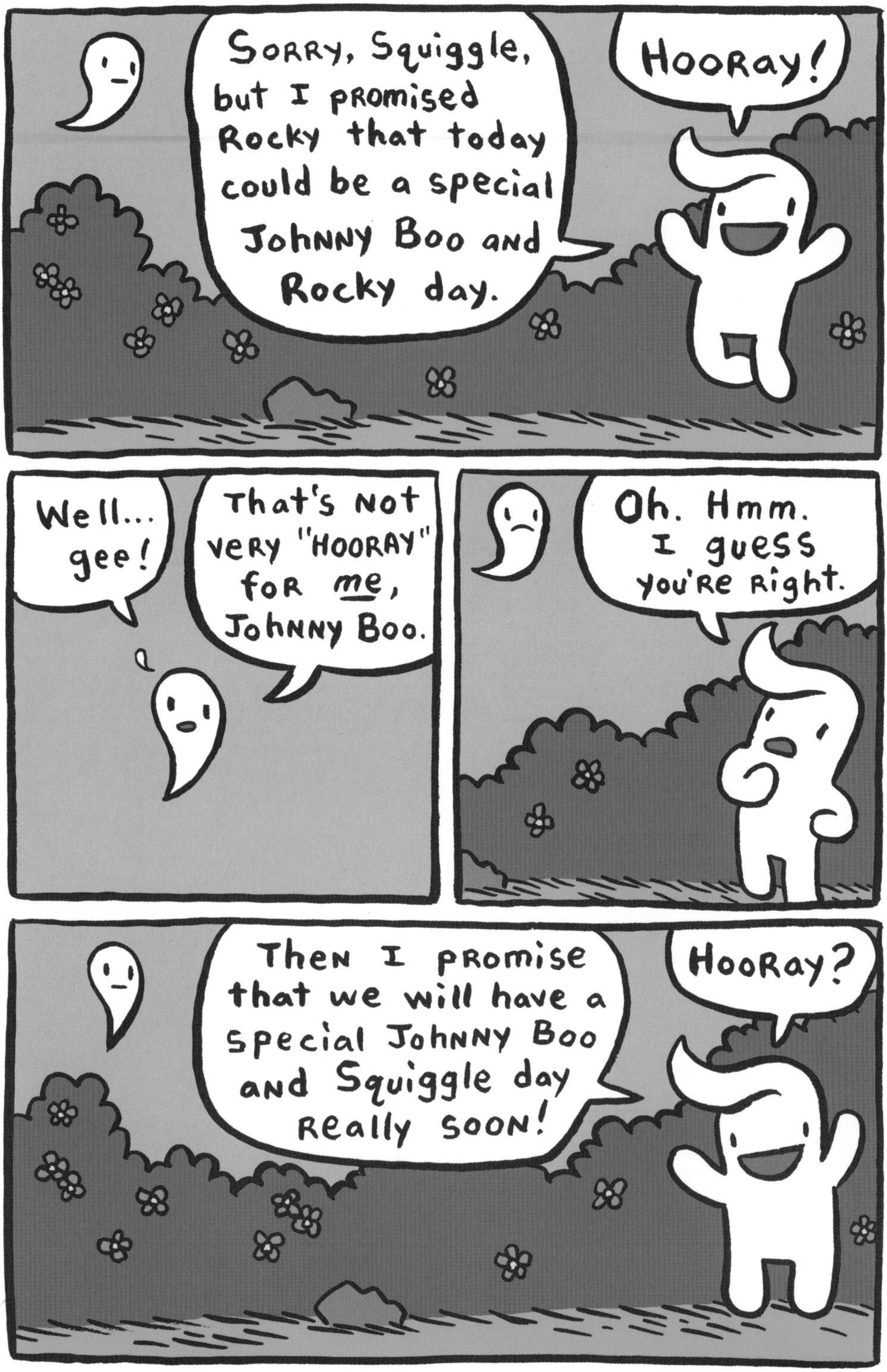
Sorry, Squiggle, but I promised Rocky that today could be a special Johnny Boo and Rocky day.
Hooray!
Well... gee!
That's not very "Hooray" for me, Johnny Boo.
Oh. Hmm. I guess you're right.
Then I promise that we will have a special Johnny Boo and Squiggle day really soon!
Hooray?

I guess so, Johnny Boo.
Good. Now say "HOORAY" so I know that you're not sad.
Hoo...
...Ray.
That's the SPIRIT, Squiggle!

CHAPTER TWO:

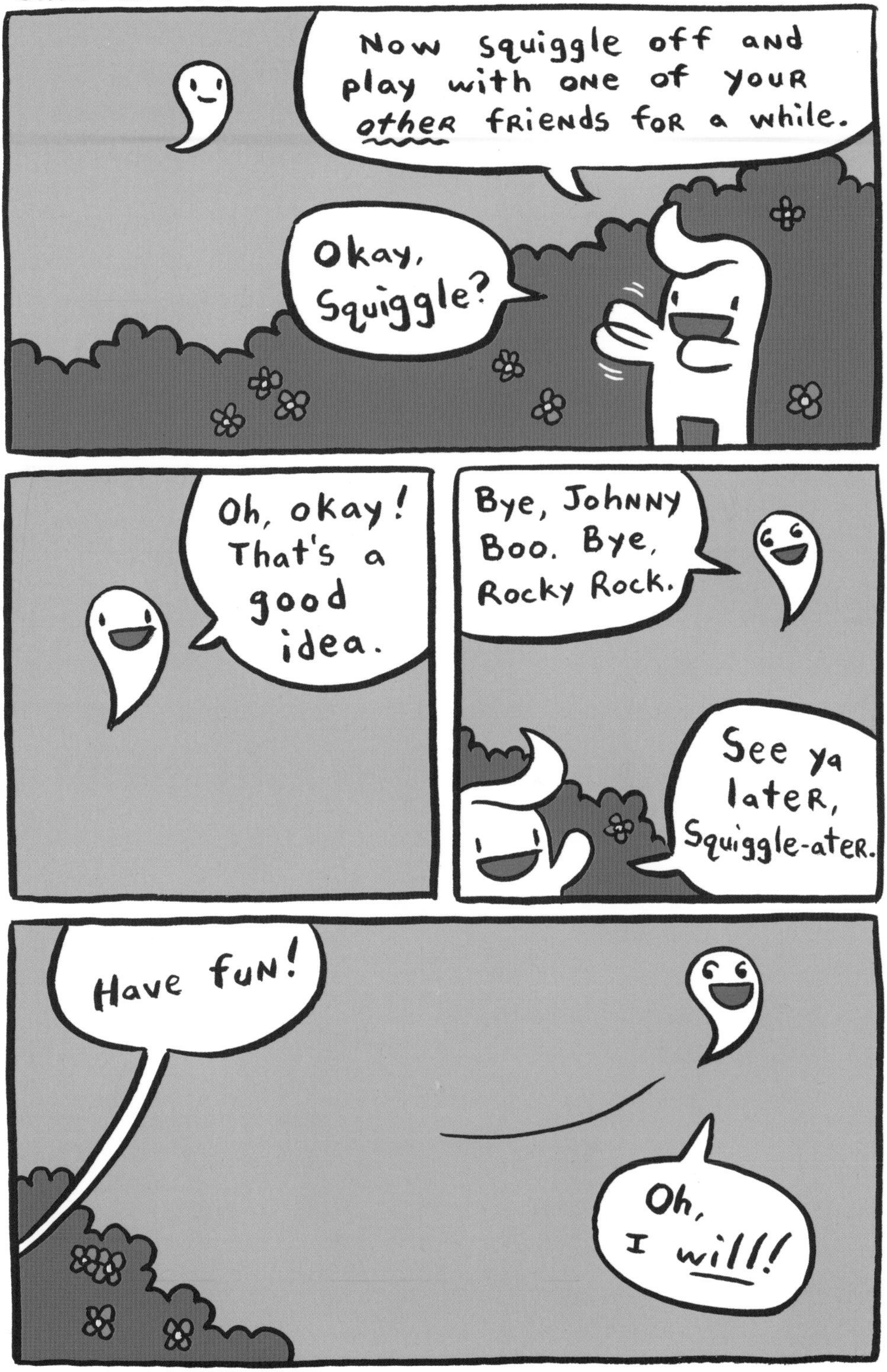

Now squiggle off and play with one of your other friends for a while.
Okay, Squiggle?
Oh, okay! That's a good idea.
Bye, Johnny Boo. Bye, Rocky Rock.
See ya later, Squiggle-ater.
Have fun!
Oh, I will!

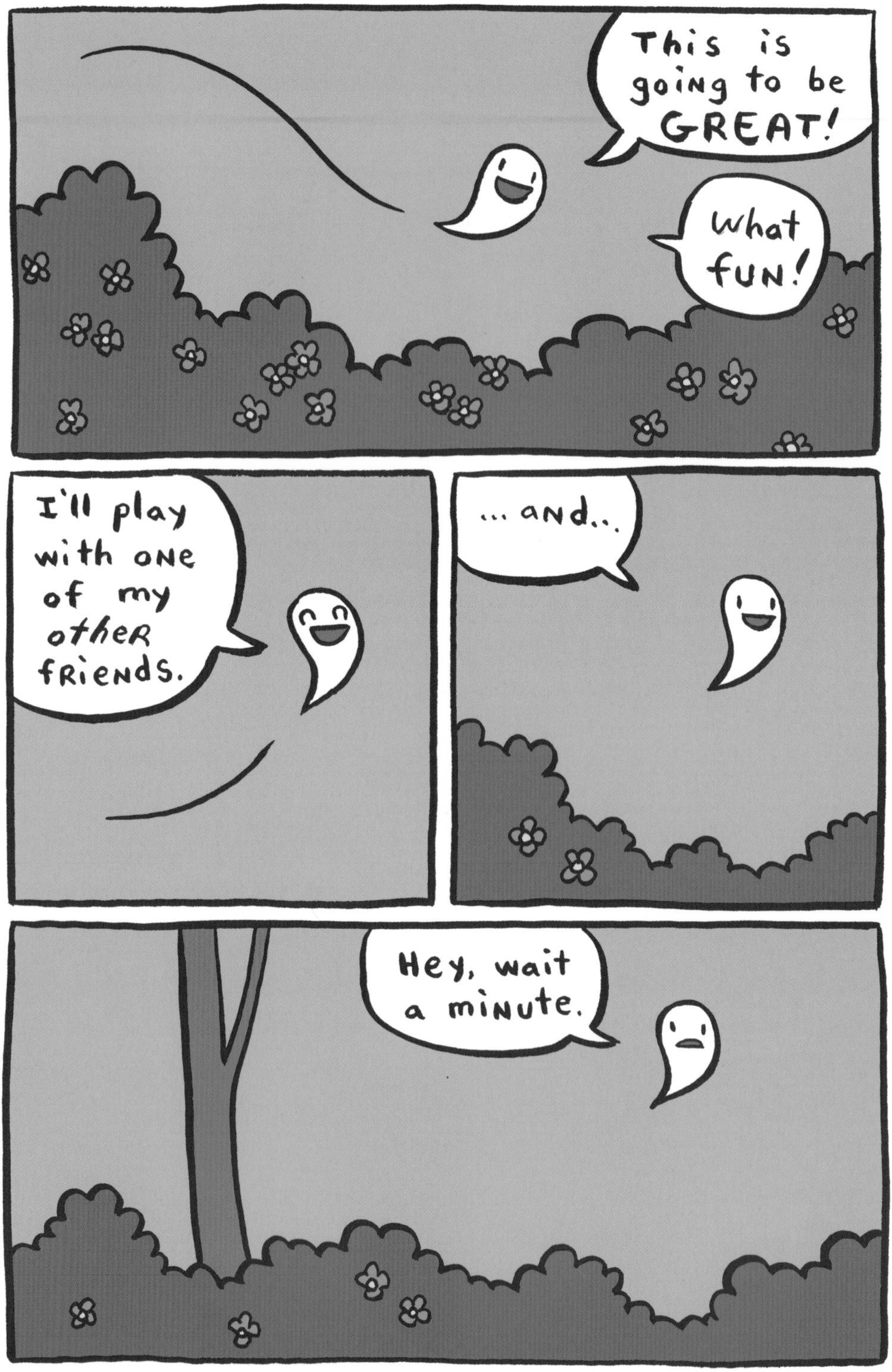
This is going to be GREAT!
What FUN!
I'll play with one of my other friends.
... and...
Hey, wait a minute.

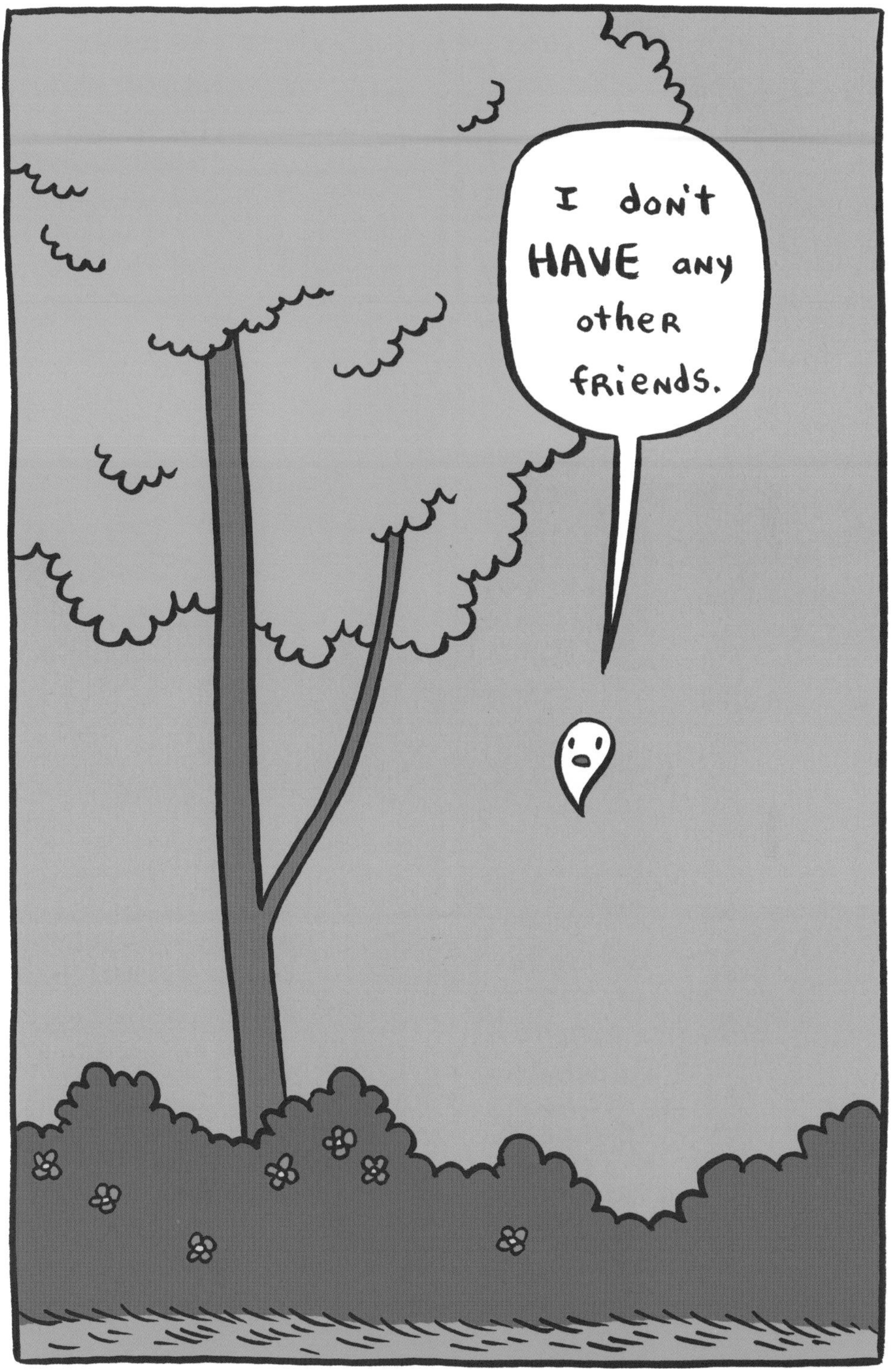
I don't HAVE any other friends.

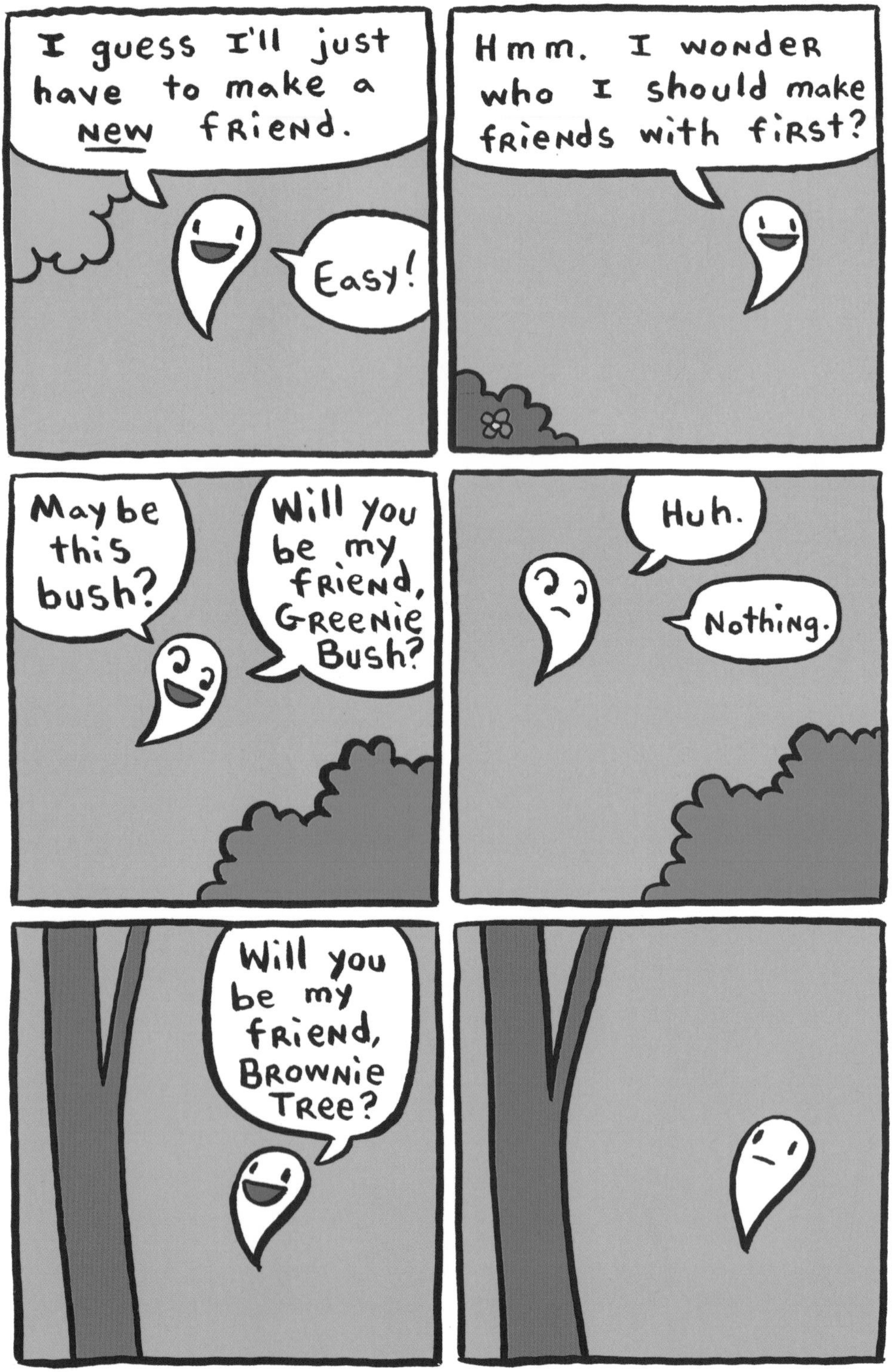
I guess I'll just have to make a NEW friend.
Easy!
Hmm. I wonder who I should make friends with first?
Maybe this bush?
Will you be my friend, Greenie Bush?
Huh.
Nothing.
Will you be my friend, Brownie Tree?

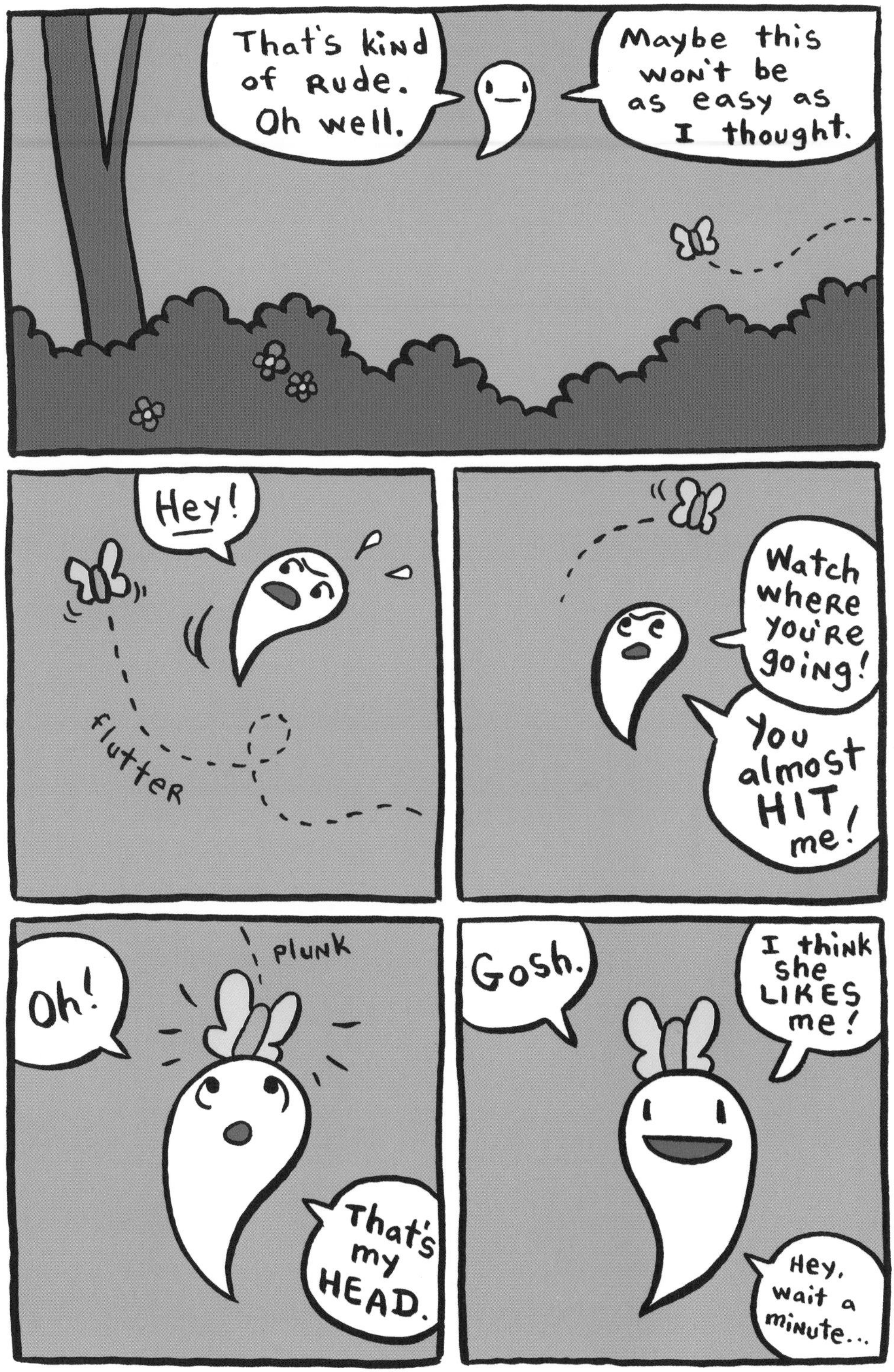
That's kind of Rude. Oh well.
Maybe this won't be as easy as I thought.
Hey!
flutter
Watch where you're going!
You almost HIT me!
Oh!
plunk
That's my HEAD.
Gosh.
I think she LIKES me!
Hey, wait a minute...

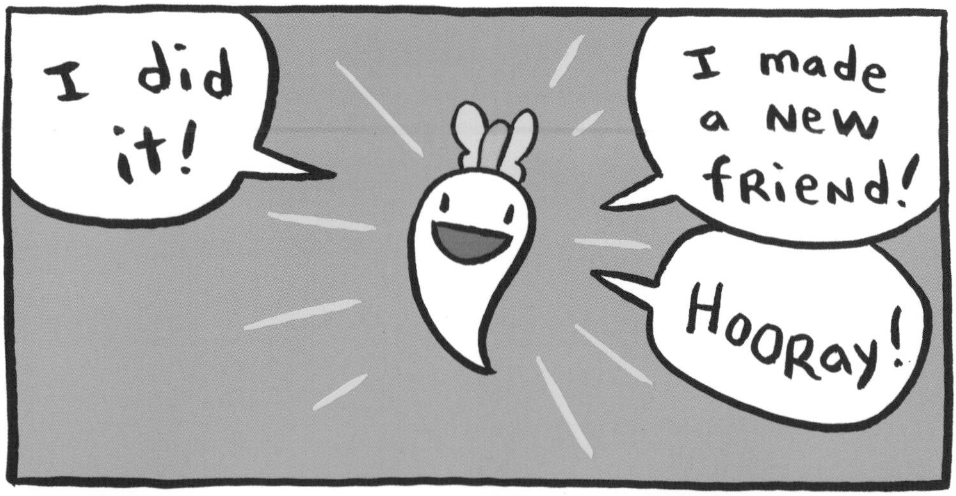
I did it!
I made a New friend!
HOORay!

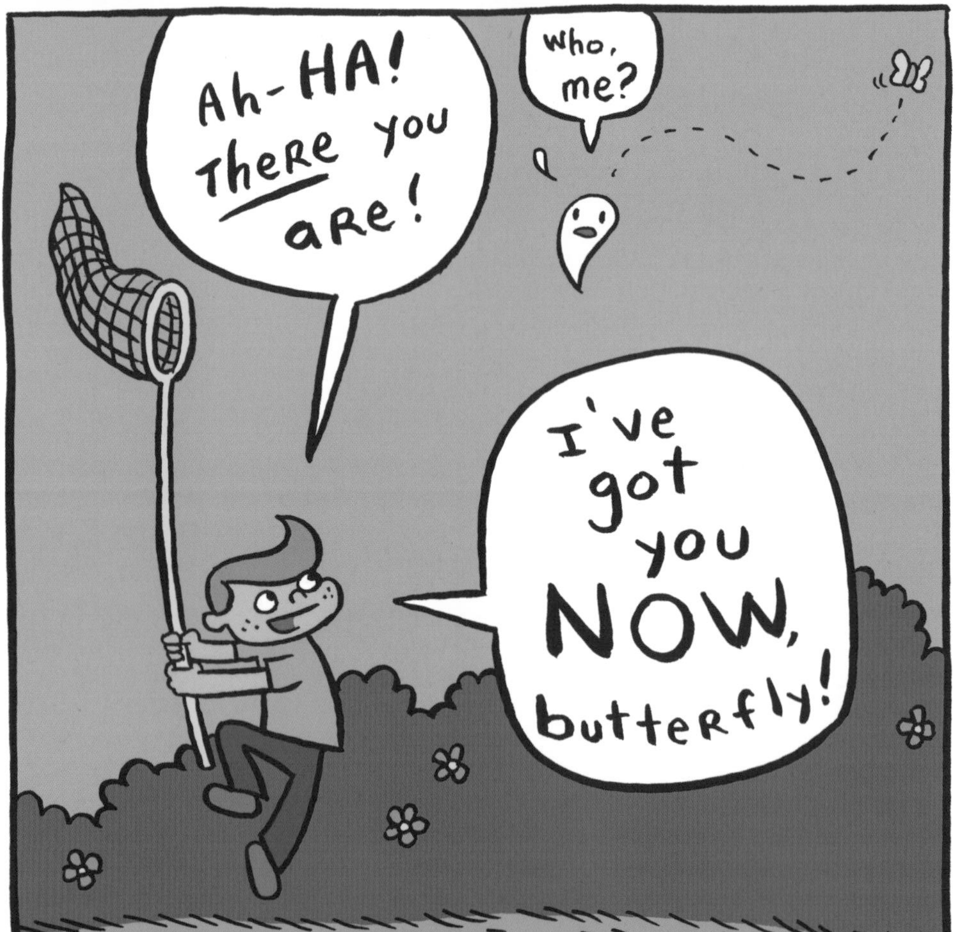
Ah-HA! There you are!
Who, me?
I've got you NOW, butterfly!

CHAPTER THREE:

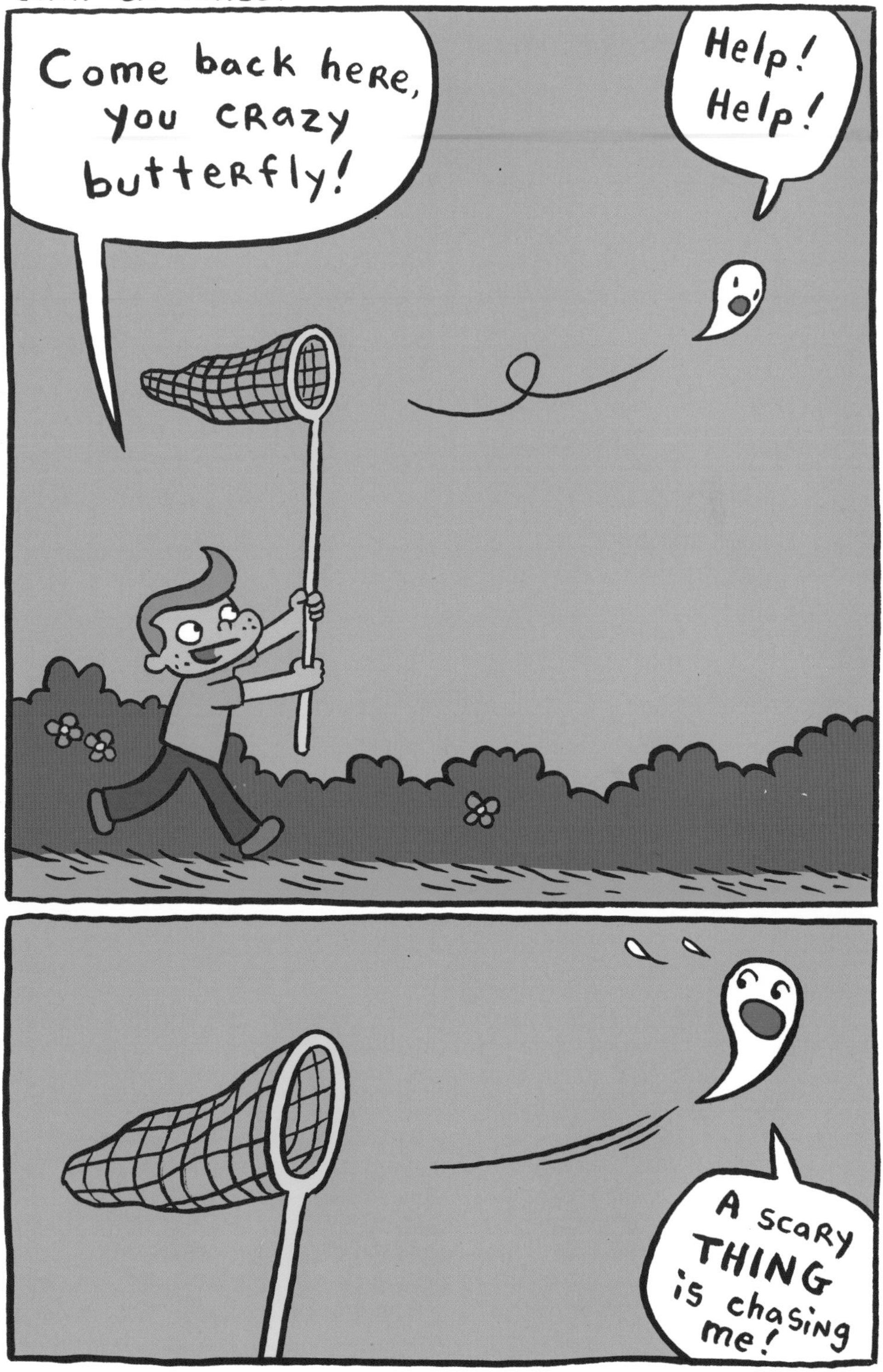
Come back here, you crazy butterfly!
Help! Help!
A scary THING is chasing me!

It's called a BUTTERFLY NET!
Now let me CATCH you!
No!
Hey! Why won't you let me?
SWISH
SWOOOOSH
Because I'm NOT a BUTTERFLY!
I'm SQUIGGLE!

But... we can be friends if you're friendly.
Do you want to play?
Yeah. I want to play.
Really? Hooray!
It's a little game called...

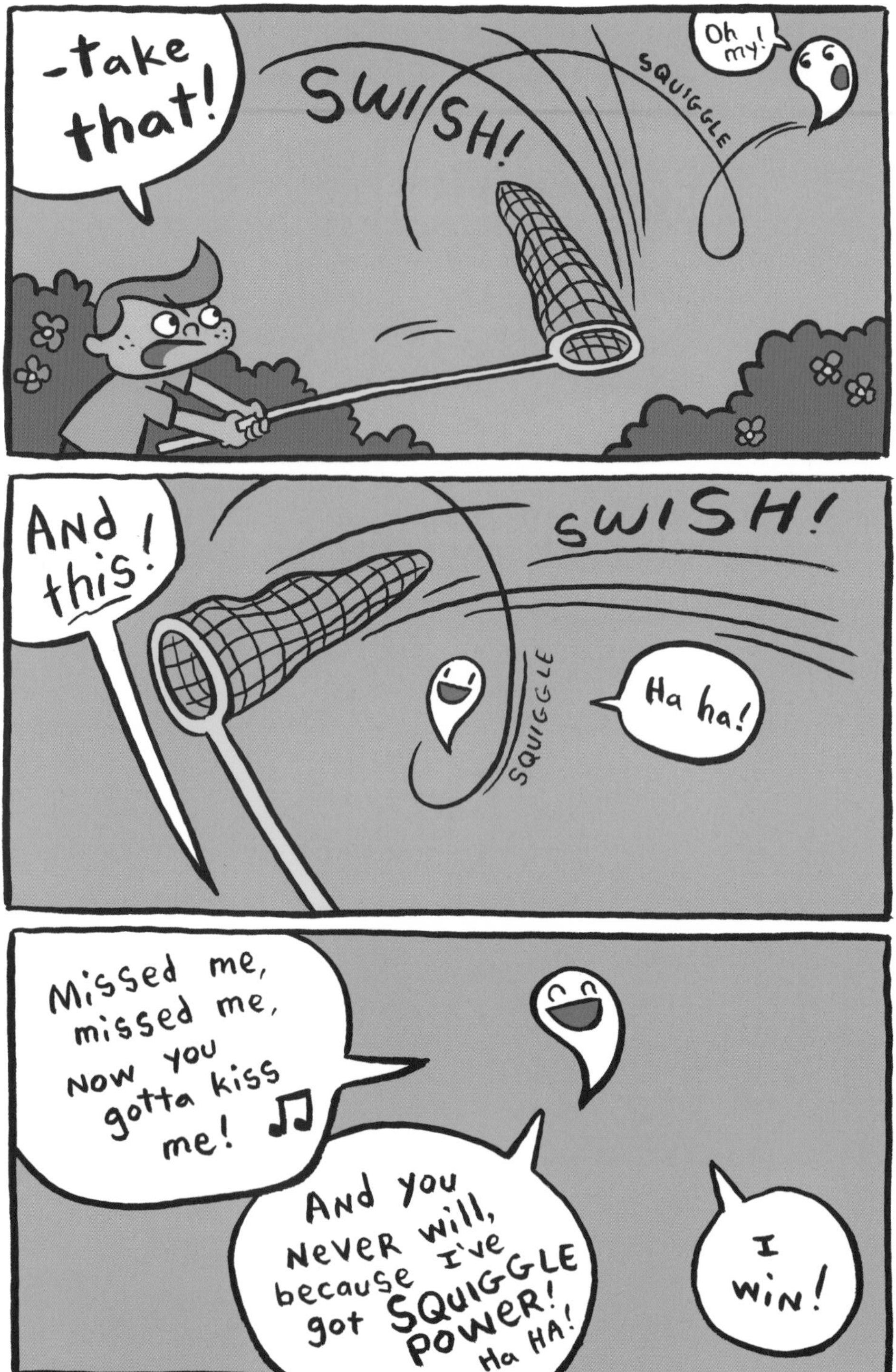
-take that!
SWISH!
SQUIGGLE
Oh my!
And this!
SWISH!
SQUIGGLE
Ha ha!
Missed me, missed me, Now you gotta kiss me! ♫
And you Never will, because I've got SQUIGGLE POWER! Ha HA!
I win!

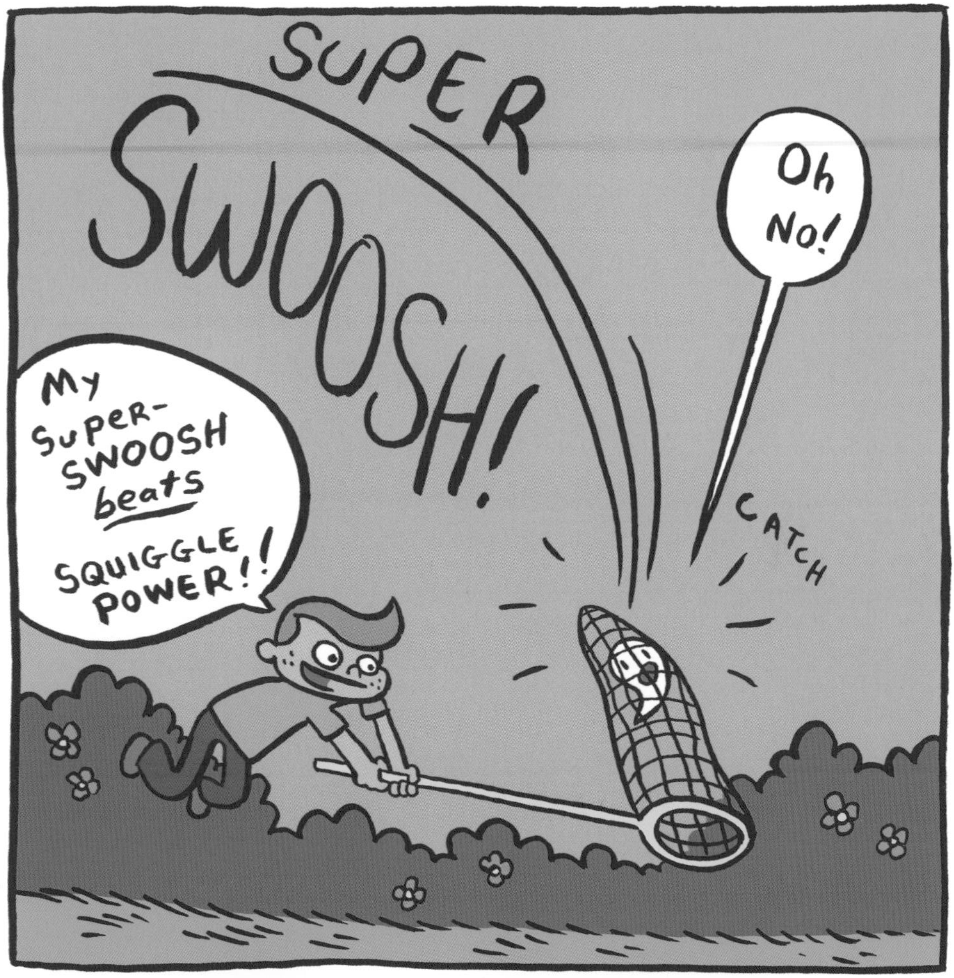
SUPER SWOOSH!
Oh No!
My Super-SWOOSH beats SQUIGGLE POWER!!
CATCH

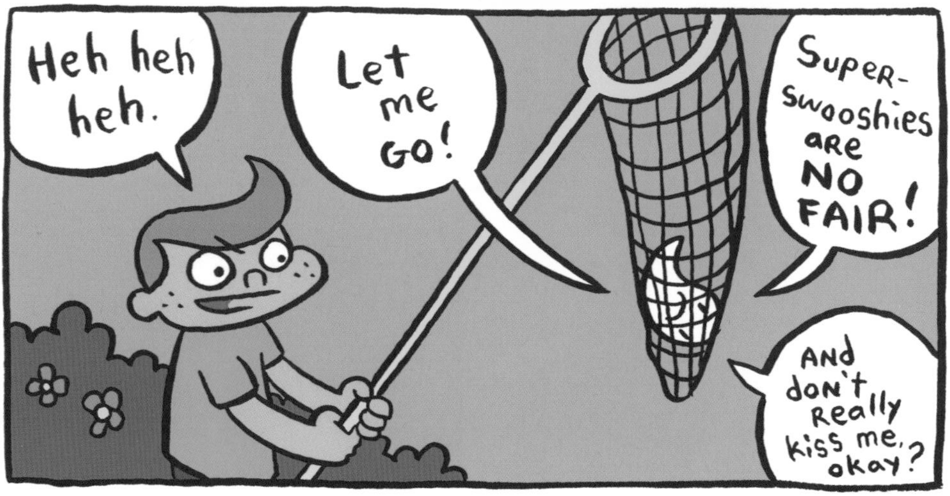
Heh heh heh.
Let me GO!
Super-Swooshies are NO FAIR!
AND don't Really kiss me, okay?

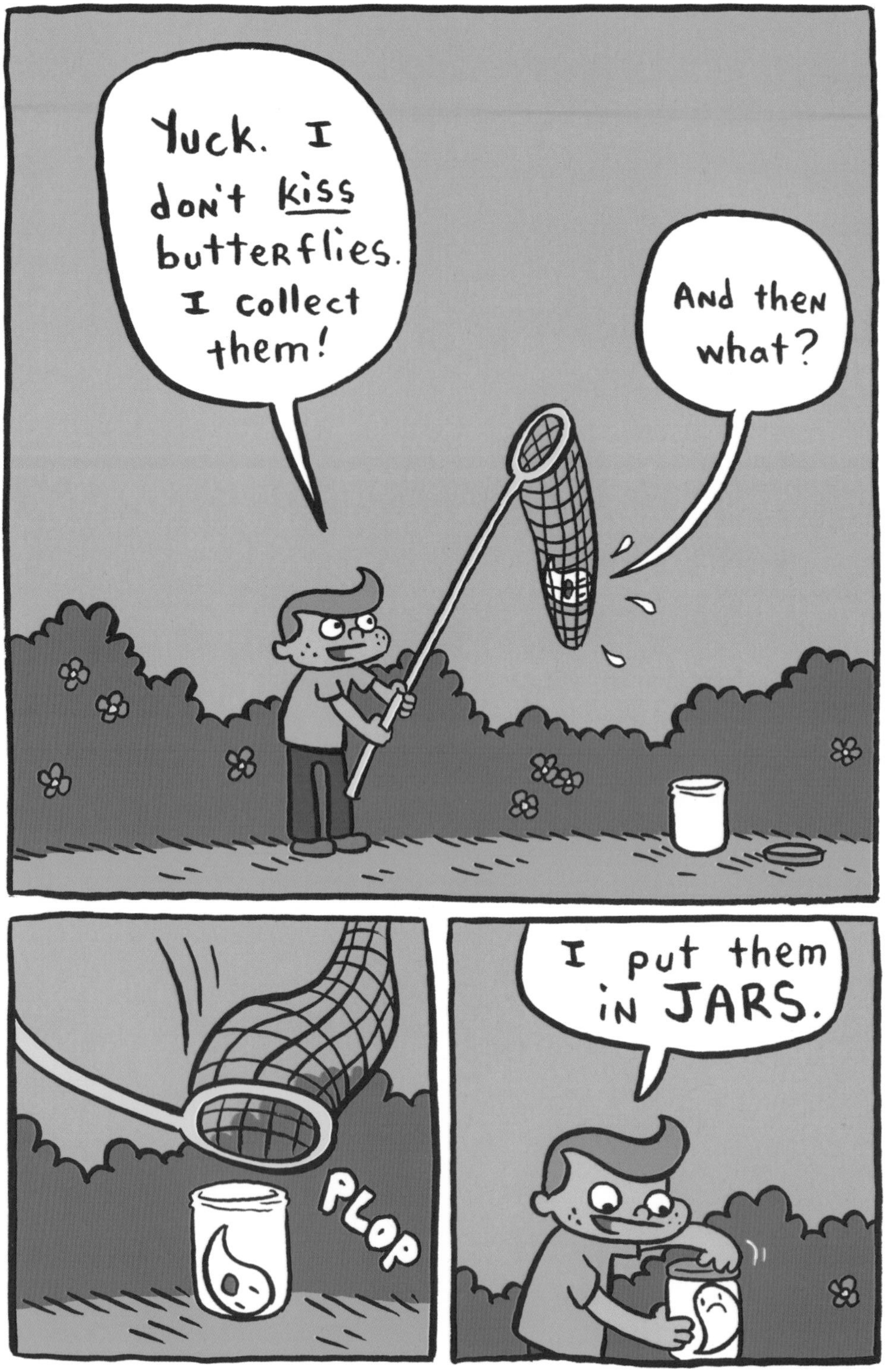
Yuck. I don't kiss butterflies. I collect them!
And then what?
PLOP
I put them in JARS.

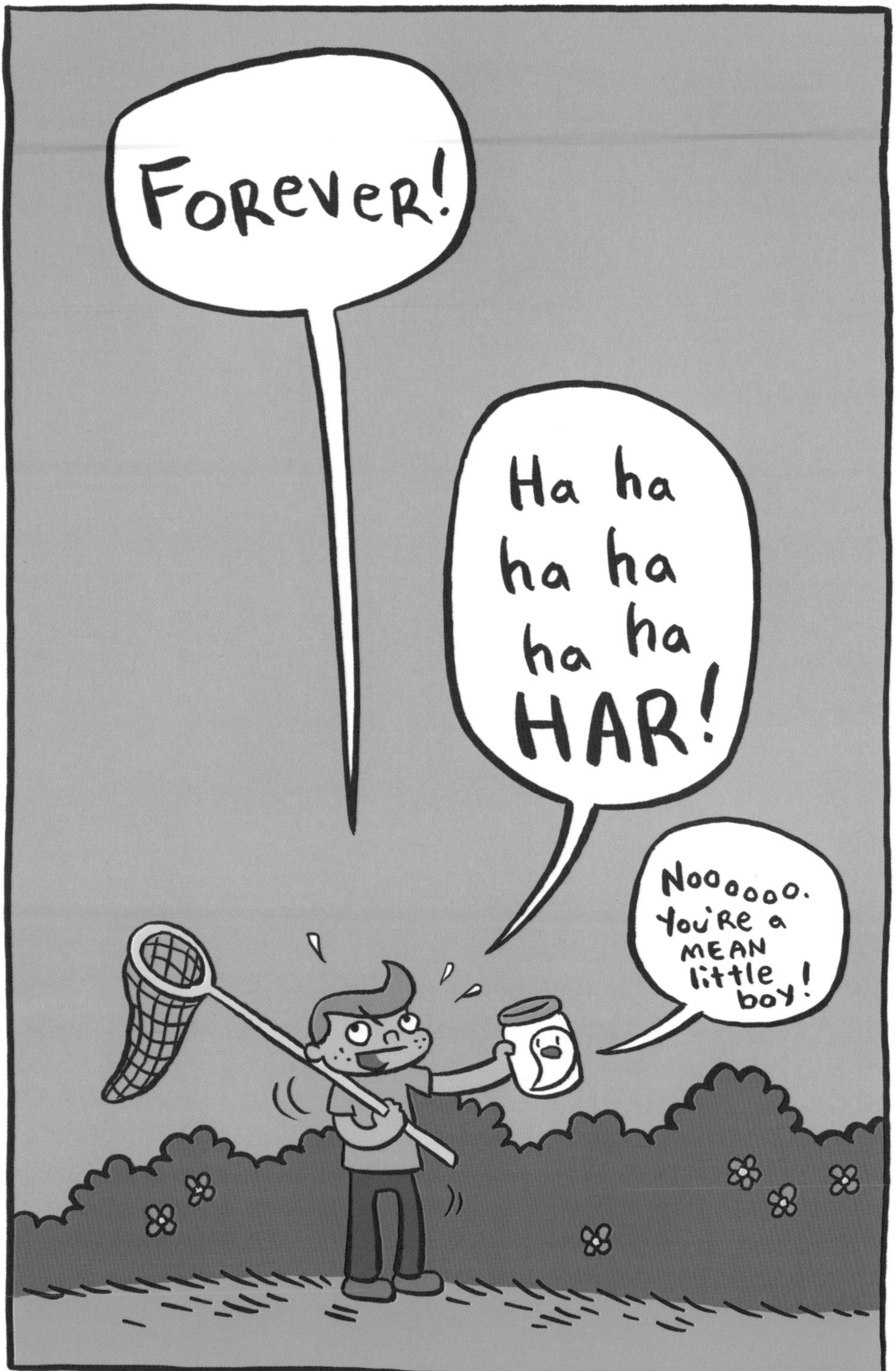
FOREVER!
Ha ha ha ha ha ha HAR!
Nooo0000. You're a MEAN little boy!

CHAPTER FOUR:

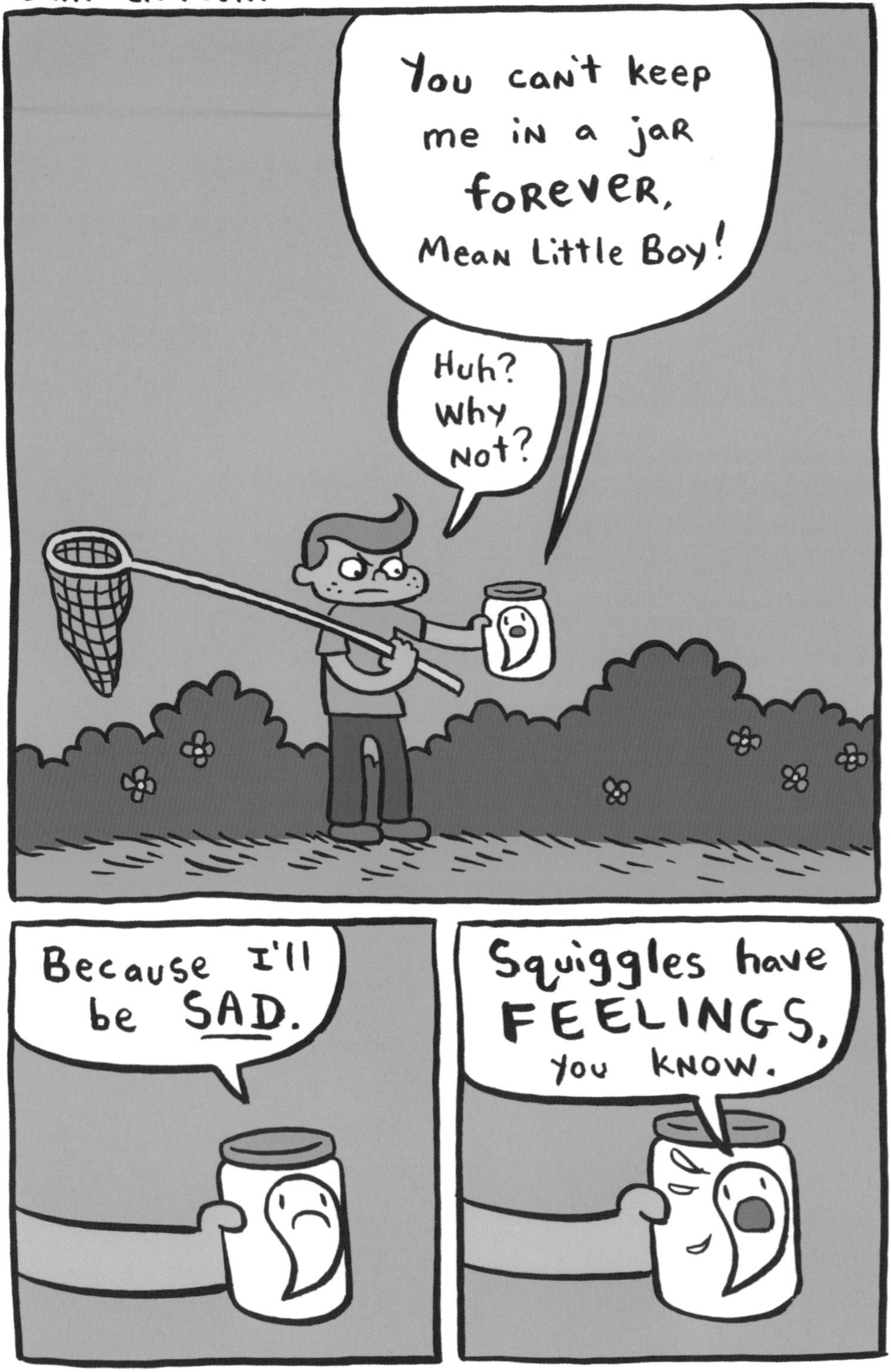
You can't keep me in a jar FOREVER, Mean Little Boy!
Huh? Why Not?
Because I'll be SAD.
Squiggles have FEELINGS, you KNOW.

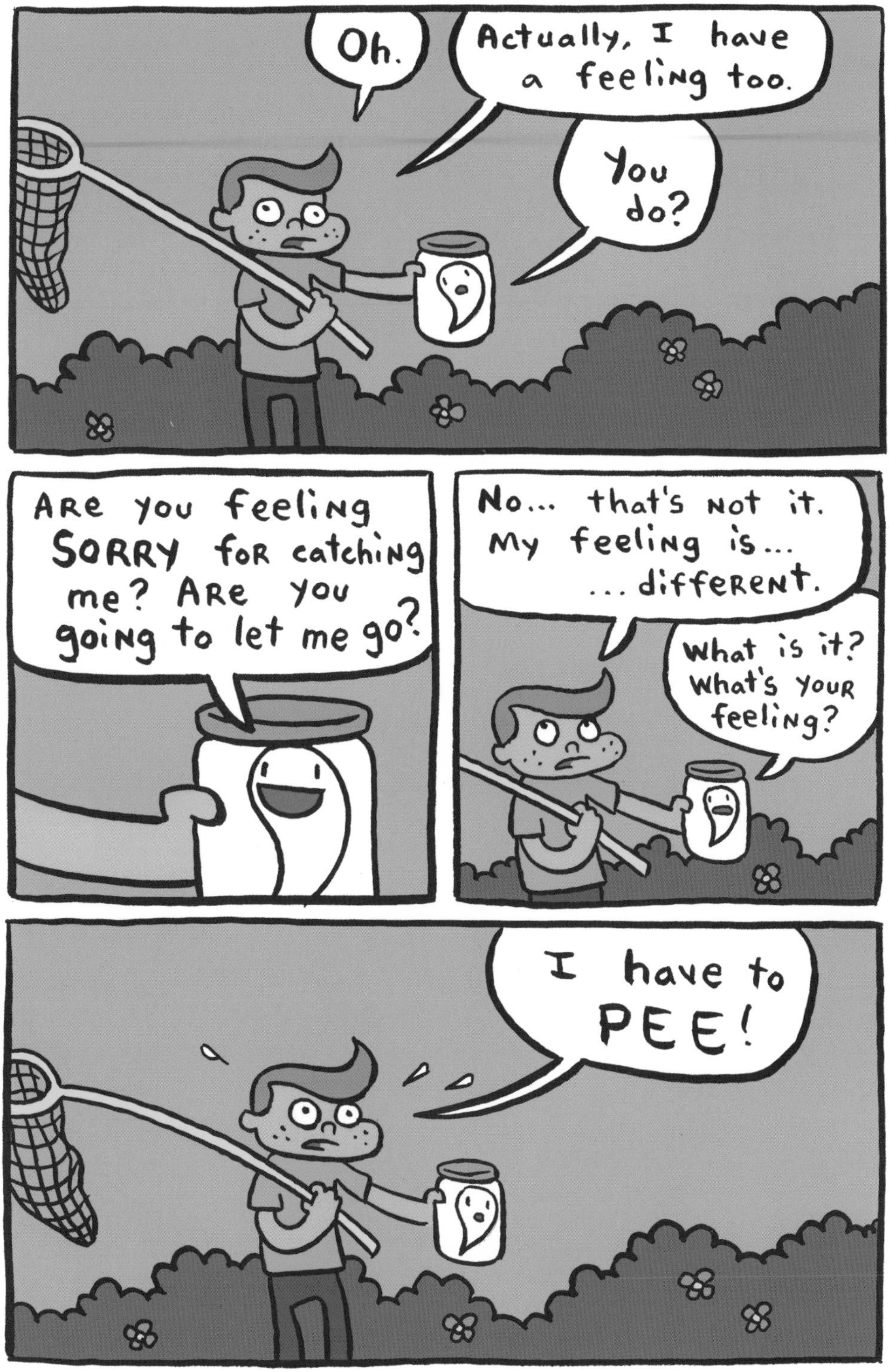
Oh.
Actually, I have a feeling too.
You do?
ARE you feeling SORRY FOR catching me? ARE you going to let me go?
No... that's NOT it. My feeling is... ...different.
What is it? What's YOUR feeling?
I have to PEE!

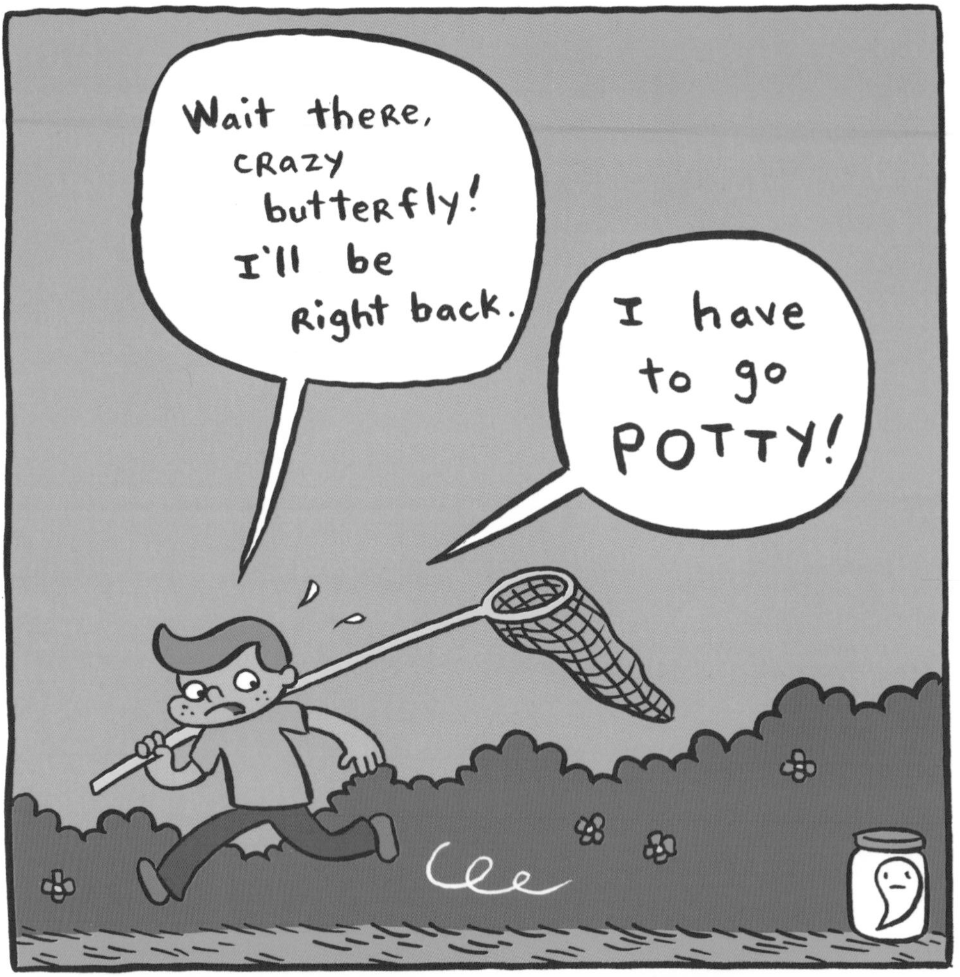
Wait there, crazy butterfly! I'll be right back.
I have to go POTTY!

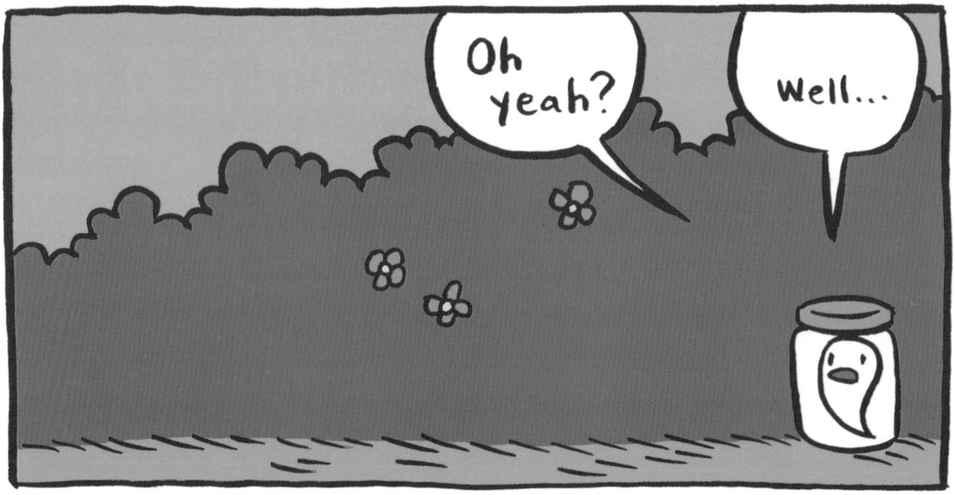
Oh yeah?
Well...

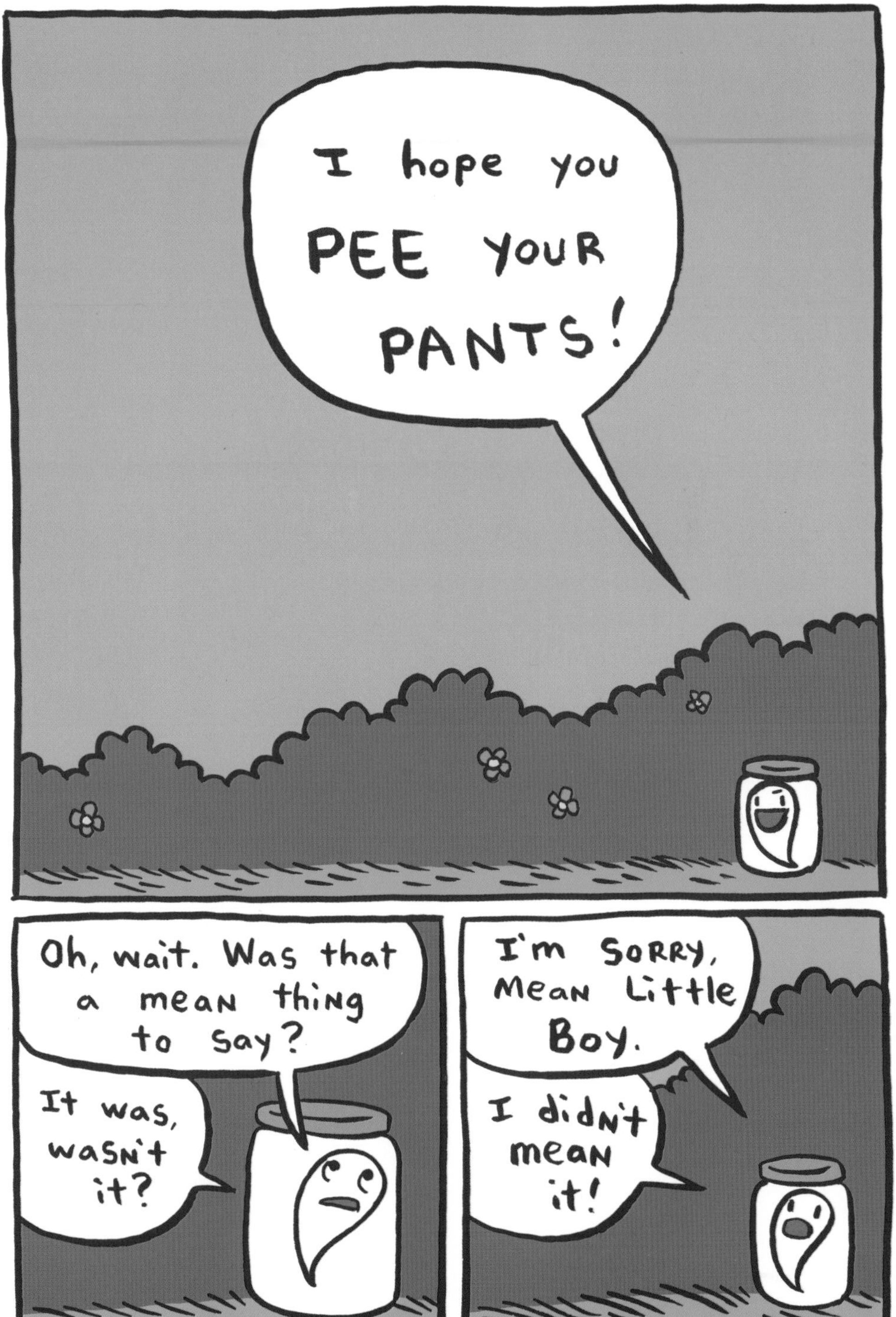
I hope you PEE YOUR PANTS!
Oh, wait. Was that a mean thing to say?
It was, wasn't it?
I'm SORRY, Mean Little Boy.
I didn't mean it!

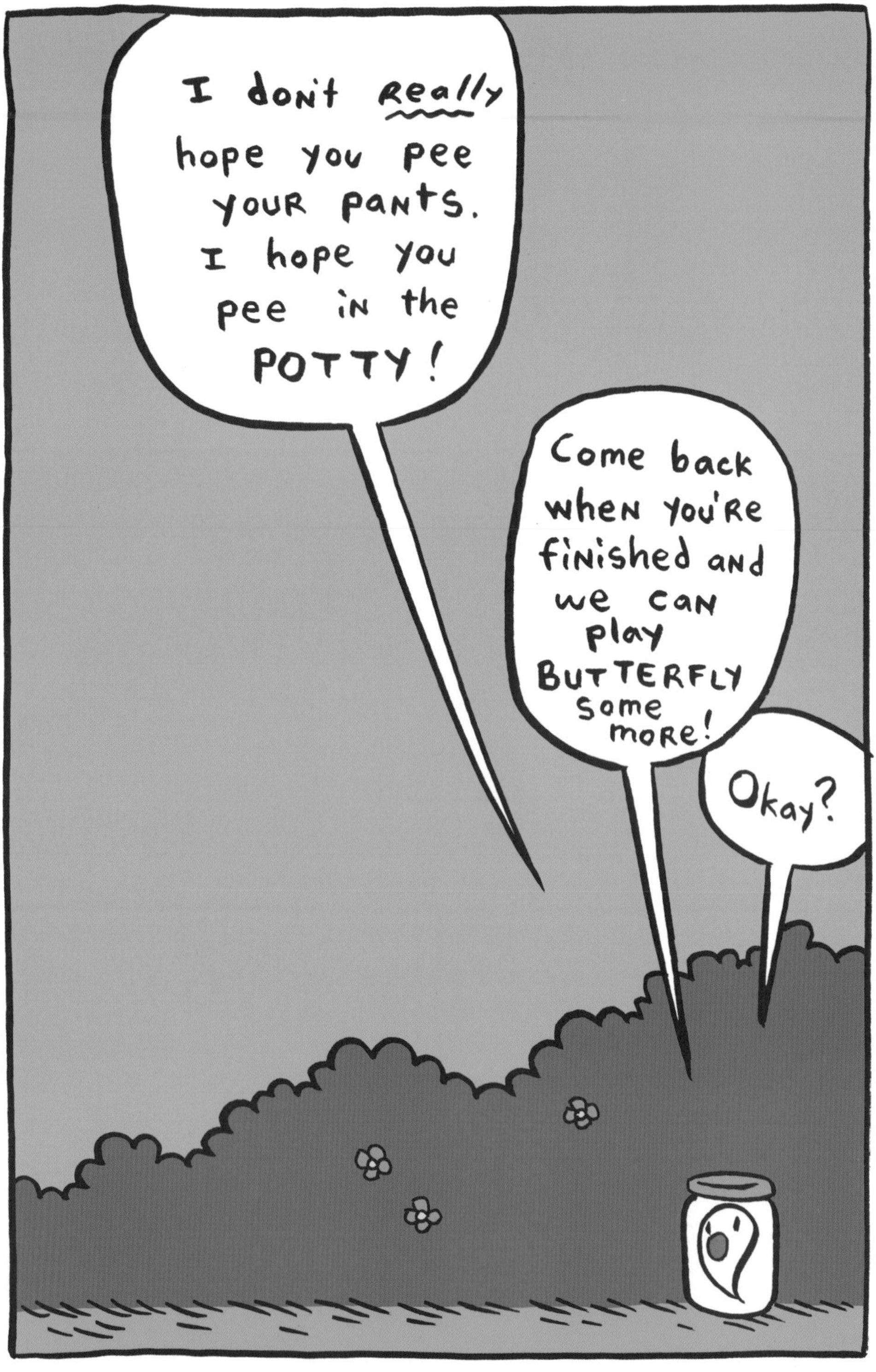
I don't really hope you pee your pants. I hope you pee in the POTTY!
Come back when you're finished and we can play BUTTERFLY some more!
Okay?

CHAPTER FIVE:

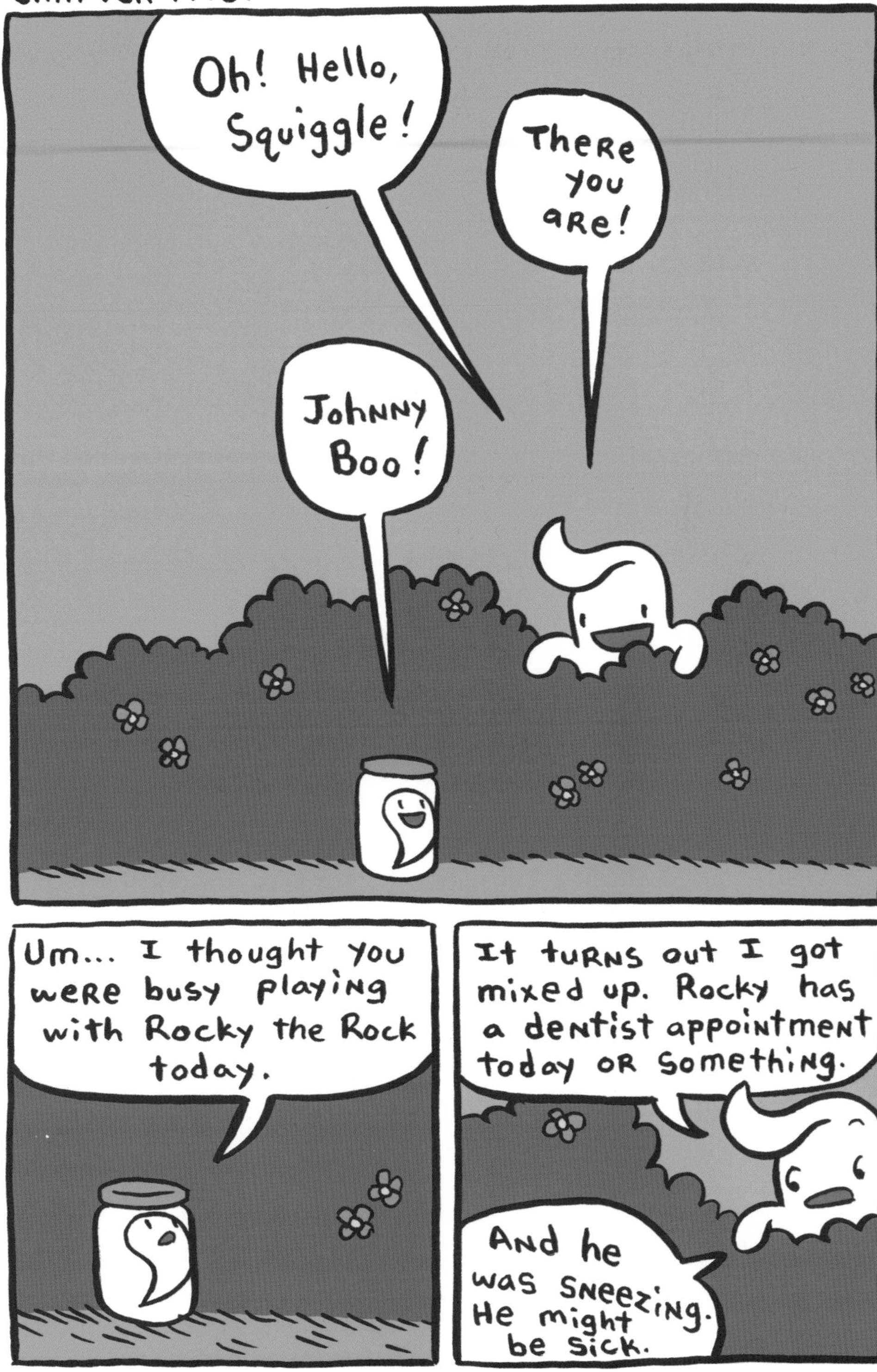

Oh! Hello, Squiggle!
There you are!
Johnny Boo!
Um... I thought you were busy playing with Rocky the Rock today.
It turns out I got mixed up. Rocky has a dentist appointment today or something.
And he was sneezing. He might be sick.

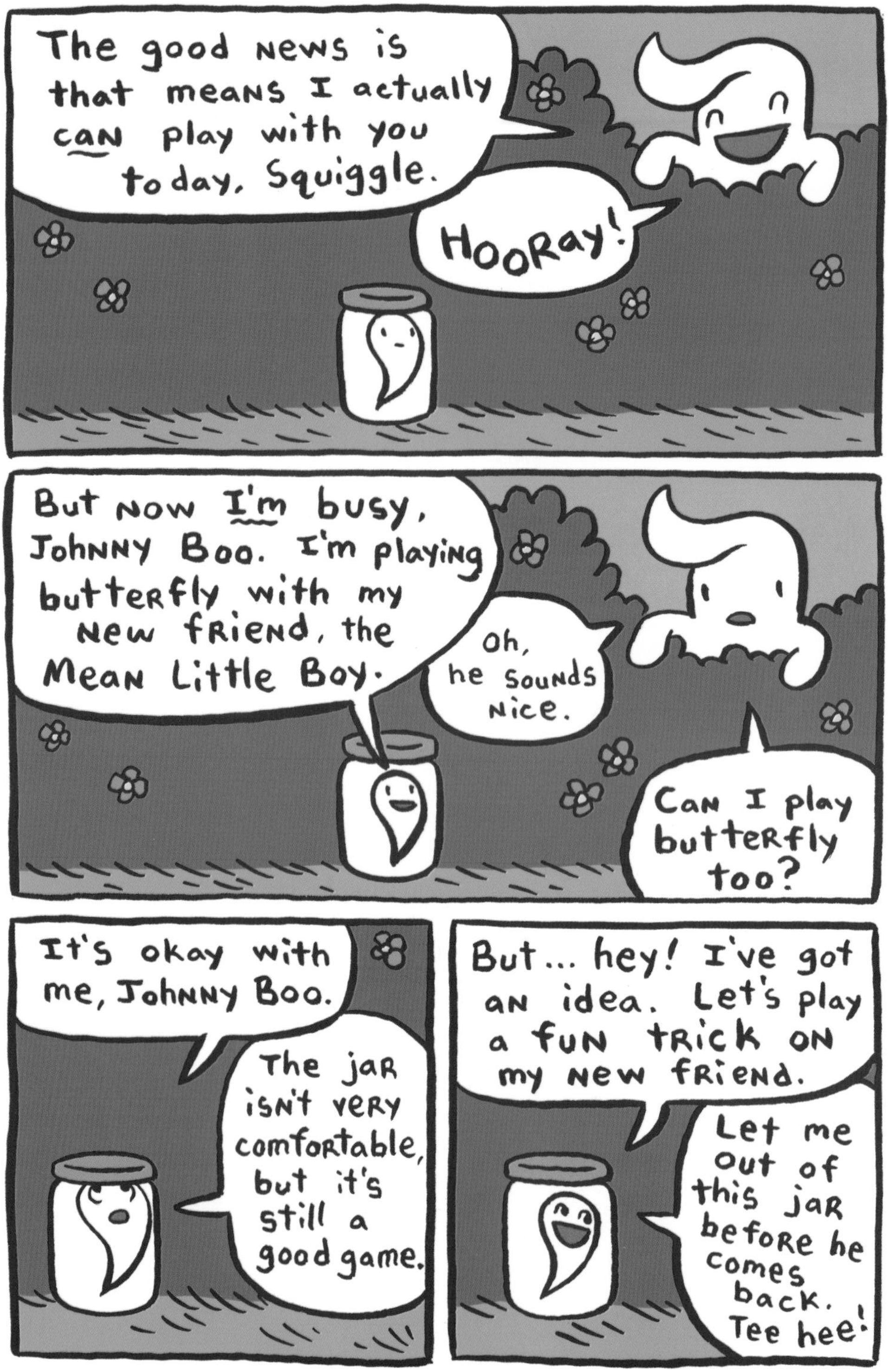
The good news is that means I actually can play with you today, Squiggle.
HOORAY!
But now I'm busy, Johnny Boo. I'm playing butterfly with my new friend, the Mean Little Boy.
Oh, he sounds nice.
Can I play butterfly too?
It's okay with me, Johnny Boo.
The jar isn't very comfortable, but it's still a good game.
But... hey! I've got an idea. Let's play a fun trick on my new friend.
Let me out of this jar before he comes back. Tee hee!

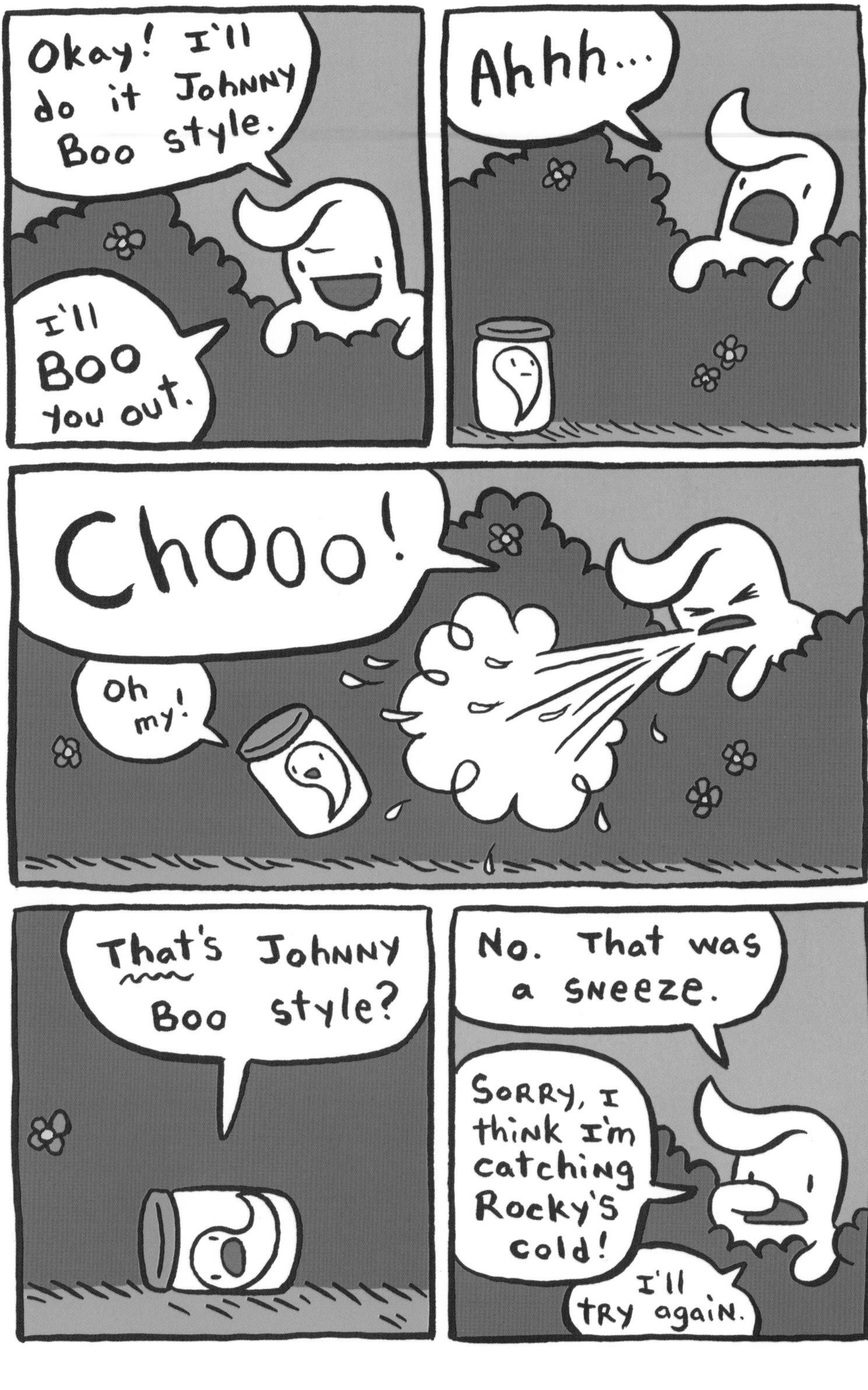
Okay! I'll do it Johnny Boo style.
I'll BOO you out.
Ahhh...
Chooo!
Oh my!
That's Johnny Boo style?
No. That was a sneeze.
Sorry, I think I'm catching Rocky's cold!
I'll try again.

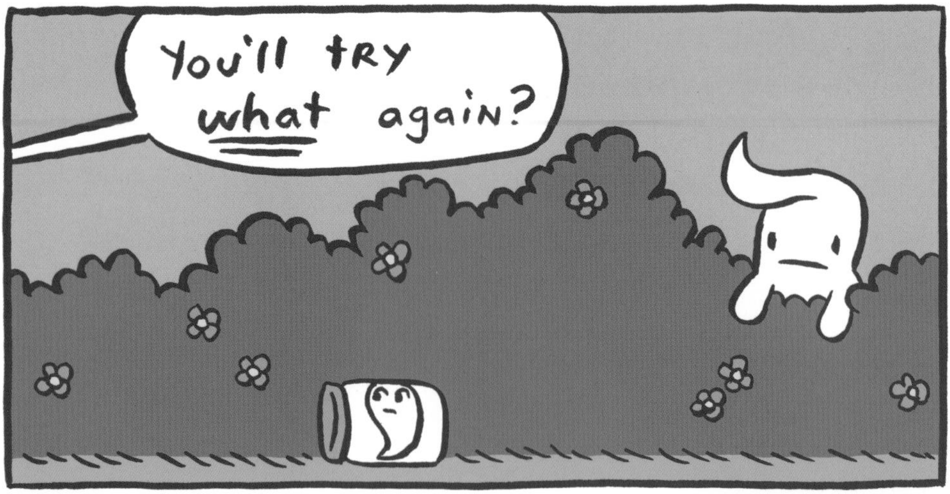
You'll try what again?

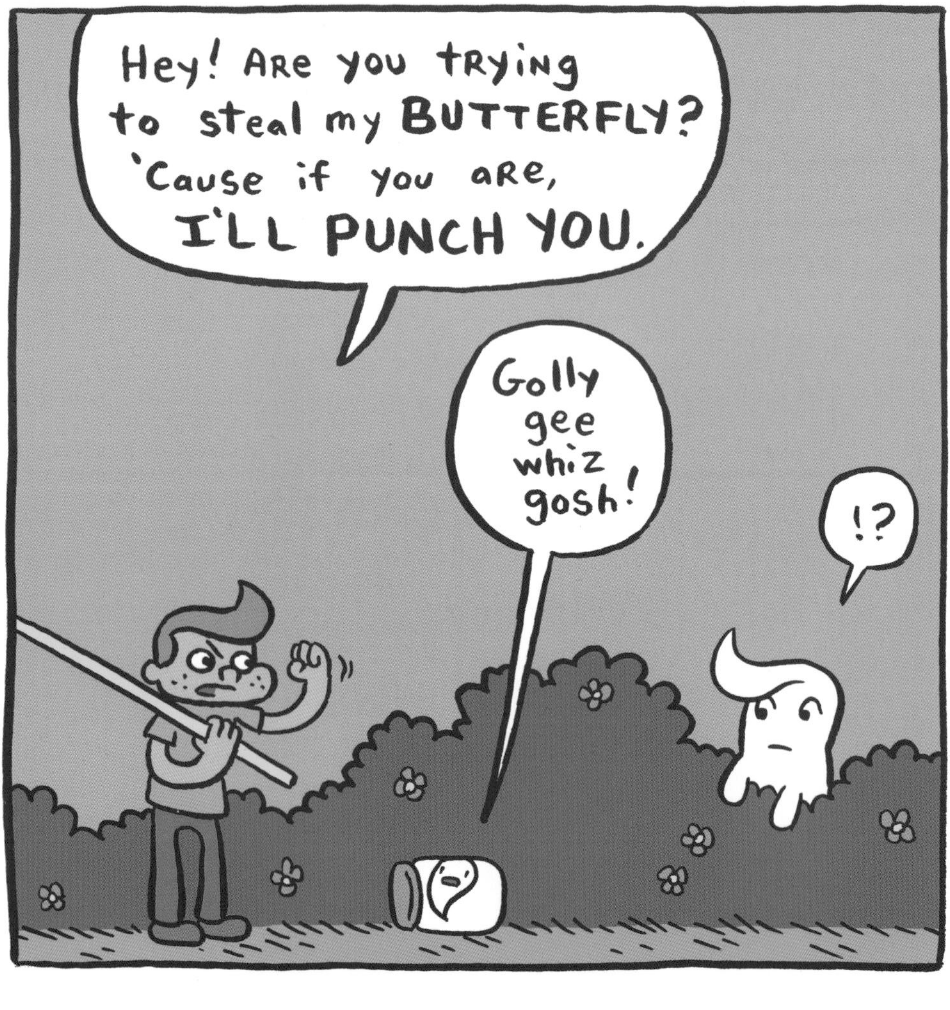
Hey! Are you trying to steal my BUTTERFLY? 'Cause if you are, I'LL PUNCH YOU.
Golly gee whiz gosh!
!?

CHAPTER SIX:

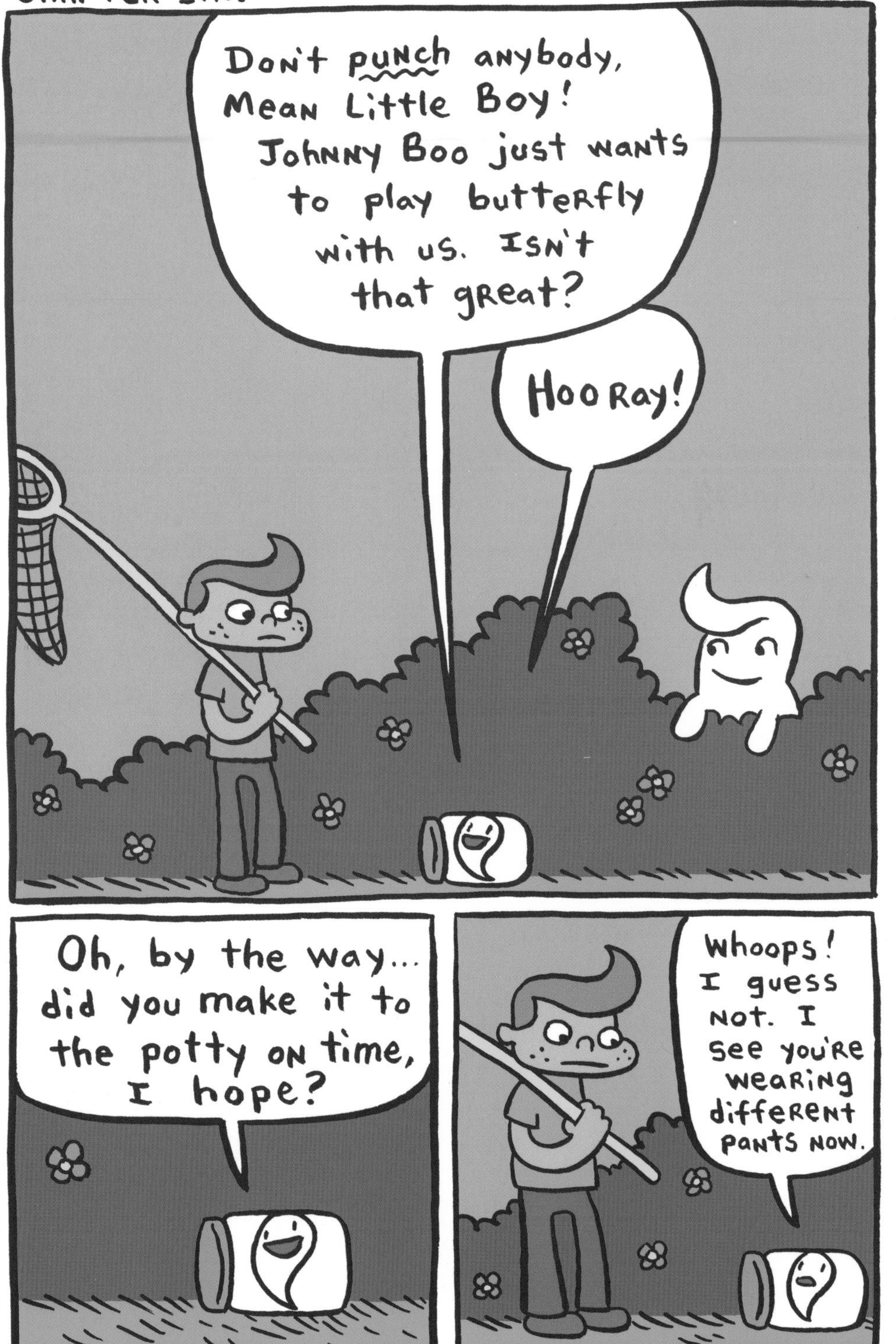

Don't punch anybody, Mean Little Boy! Johnny Boo just wants to play butterfly with us. Isn't that great?
Hooray!
Oh, by the way... did you make it to the potty on time, I hope?
Whoops! I guess not. I see you're wearing different pants now.

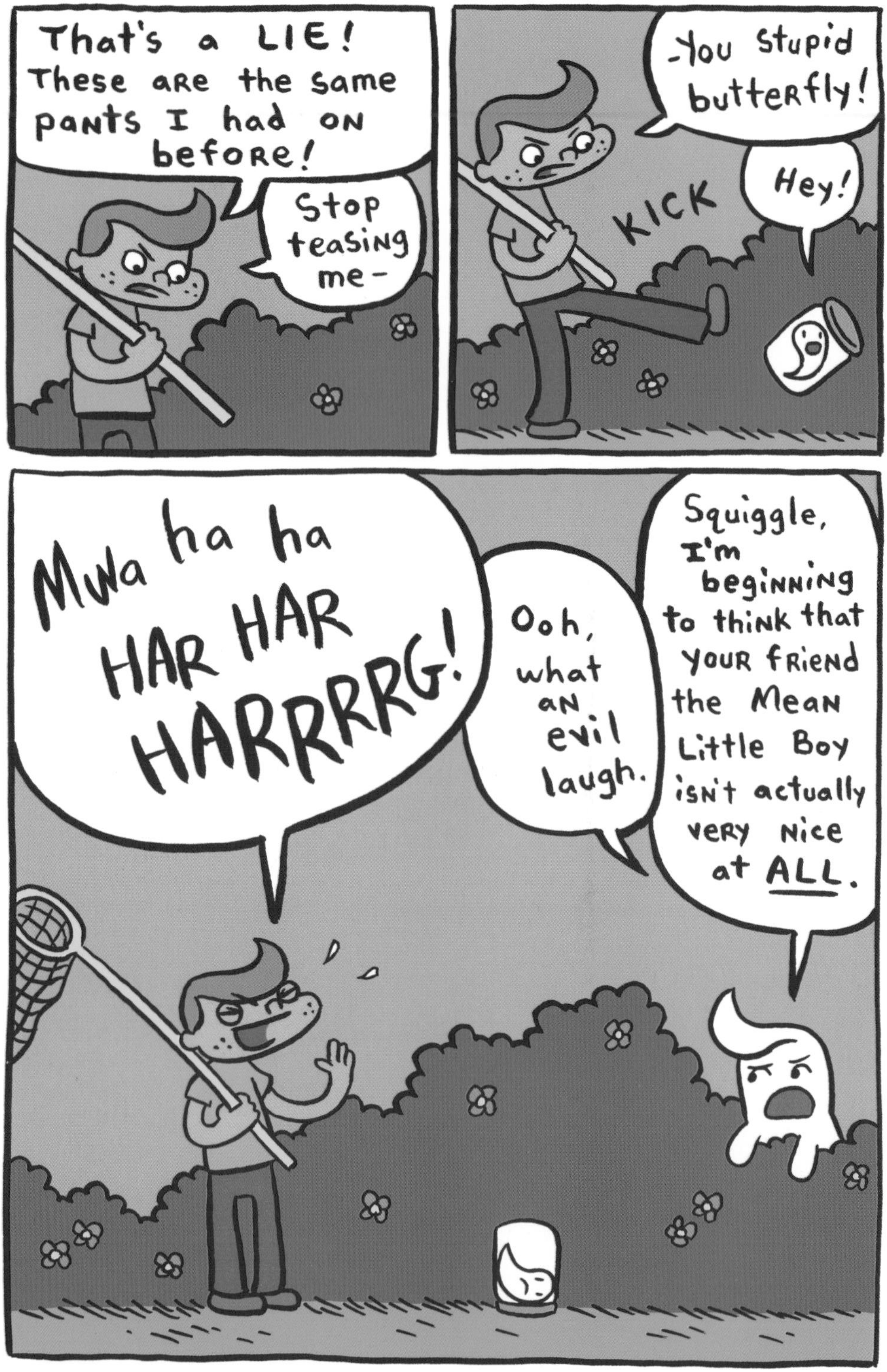

That's a LIE! These are the same pants I had on before!
Stop teasing me-
-You stupid butterfly!
KICK
Hey!
Mwa ha ha HAR HAR HARRRRG!
Ooh, what an evil laugh.
Squiggle, I'm beginning to think that your friend the Mean Little Boy isn't actually very nice at ALL.

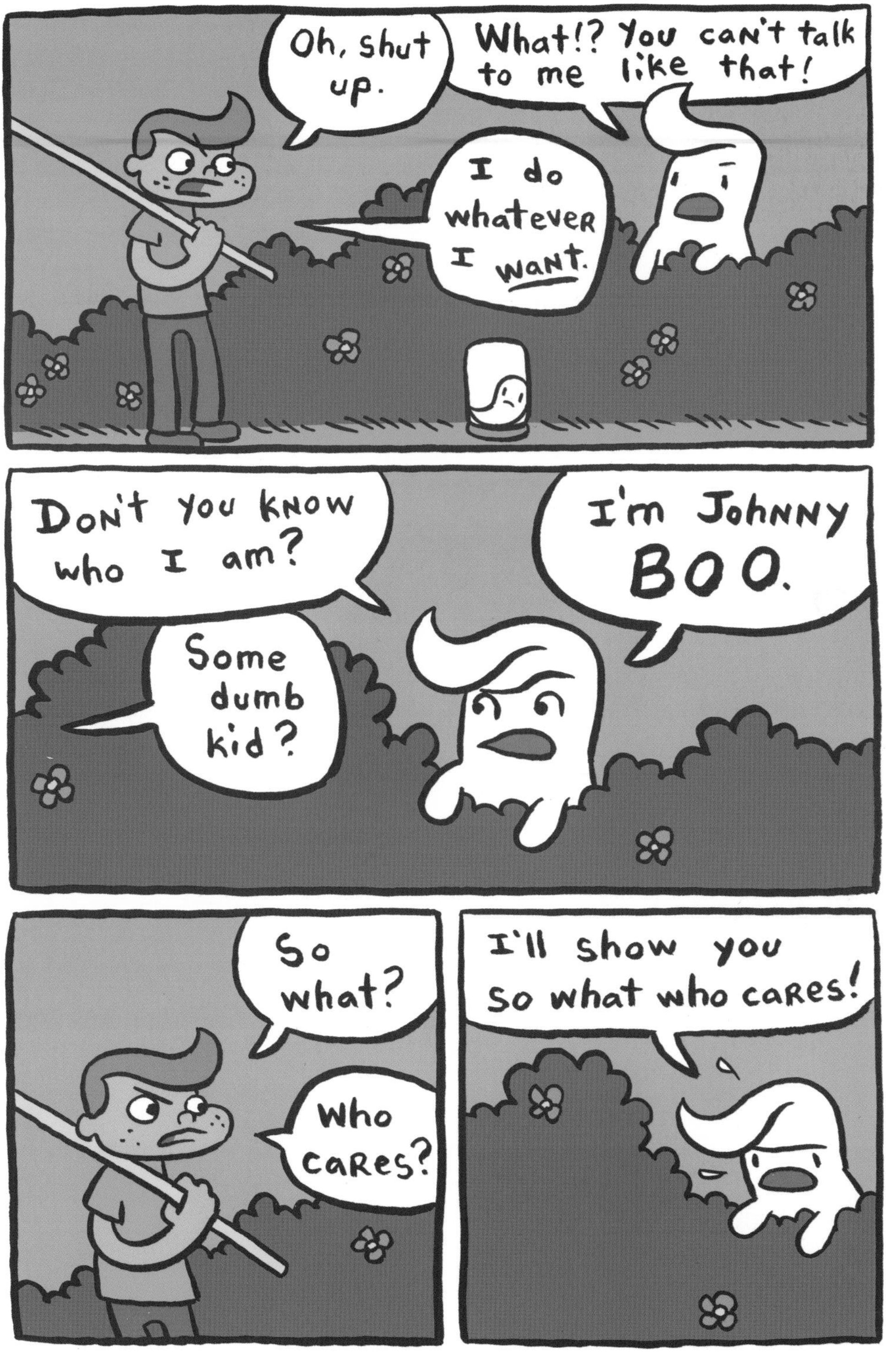
Oh, shut up.
What!? You can't talk to me like that!
I do whatever I WANT.
Don't you know who I am?
I'm Johnny BOO.
Some dumb kid?
So what?
Who cares?
I'll show you so what who cares!

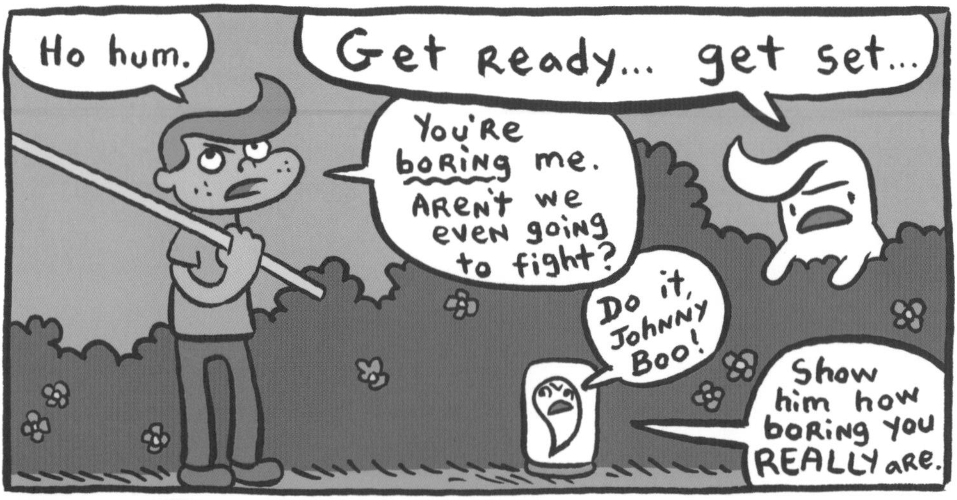
Ho hum.
Get Ready... get set...
You're boring me. Aren't we even going to fight?
Do it, Johnny Boo!
Show him how boring you REALLY are.

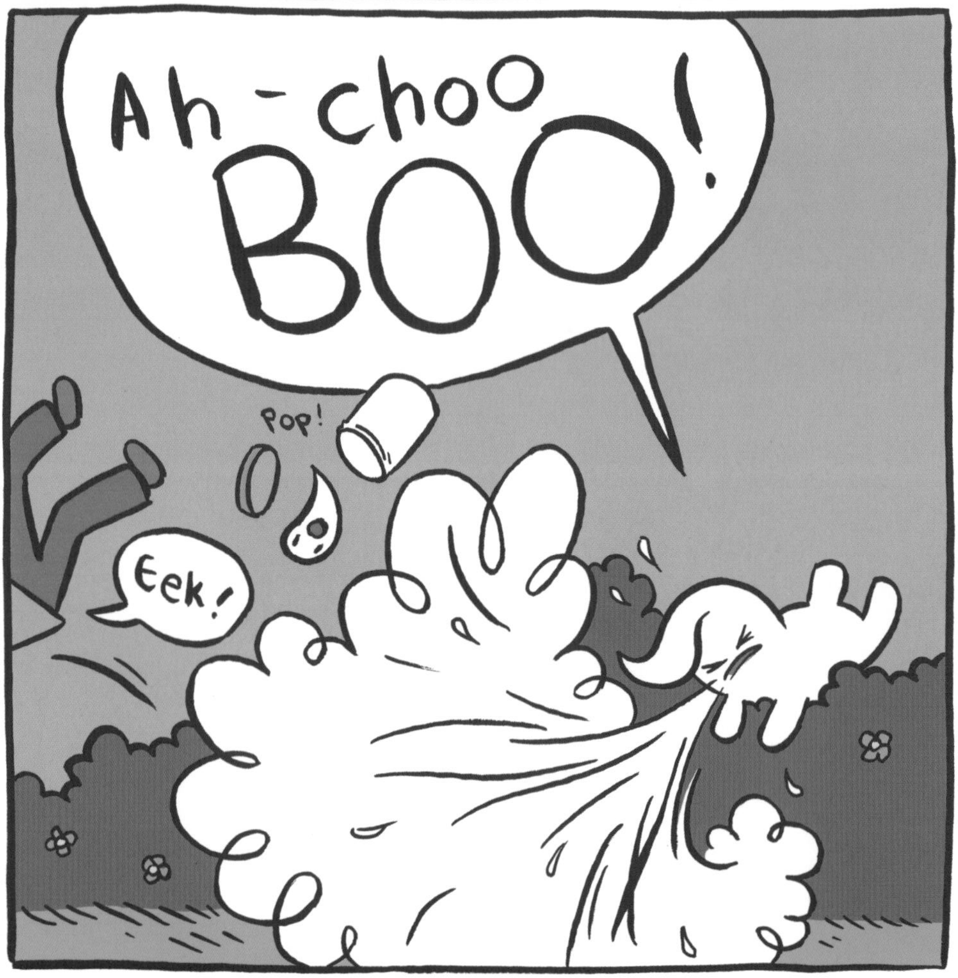
Ah-choo BOO!
POP!
Eek!

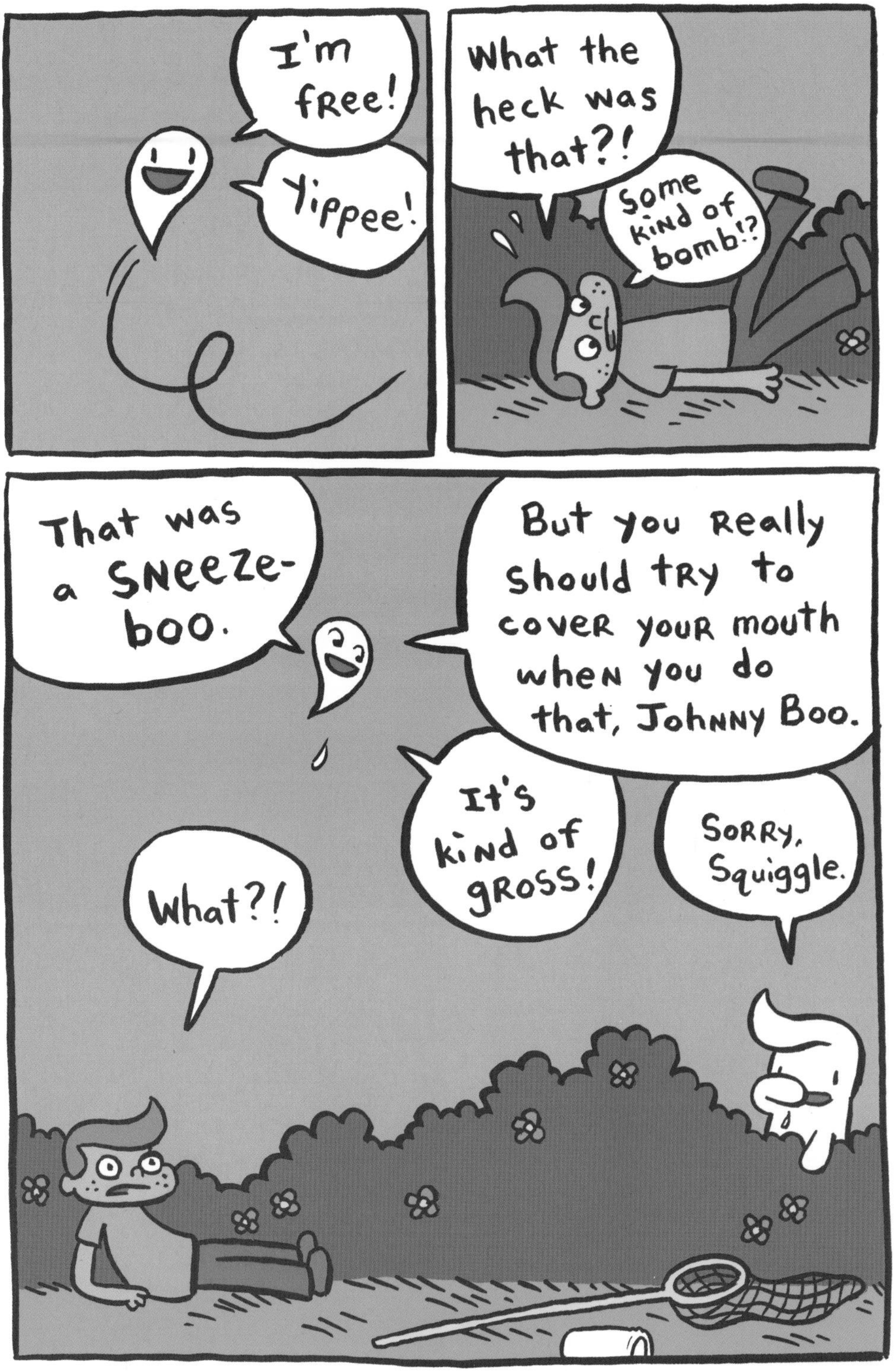
I'm free!
Yippee!
What the heck was that?!
Some kind of bomb!?
That was a SNEEZE-a-boo.
But you really should try to cover your mouth when you do that, Johnny Boo.
It's kind of gross!
What?!
Sorry, Squiggle.

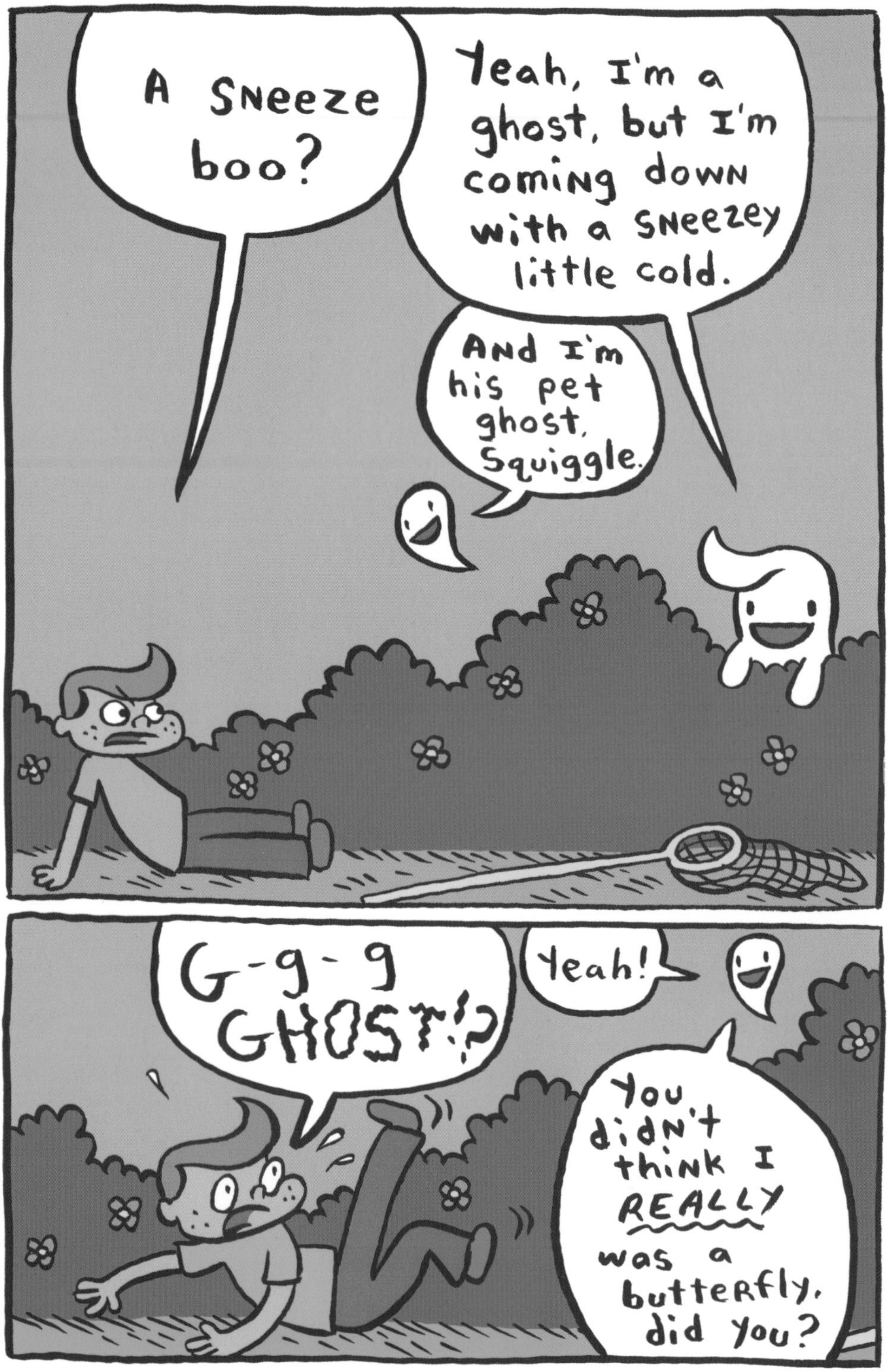
A Sneeze boo?
Yeah, I'm a ghost, but I'm coming down with a sneezey little cold.
And I'm his pet ghost, Squiggle.
G-g-g GHOST!?
Yeah!
You didn't think I REALLY was a butterfly, did you?

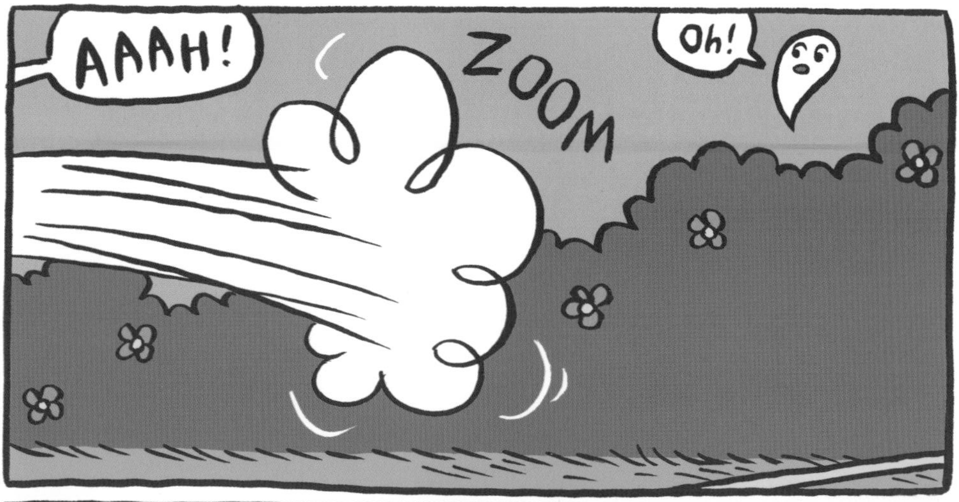
AAAH!
ZOOM
Oh!

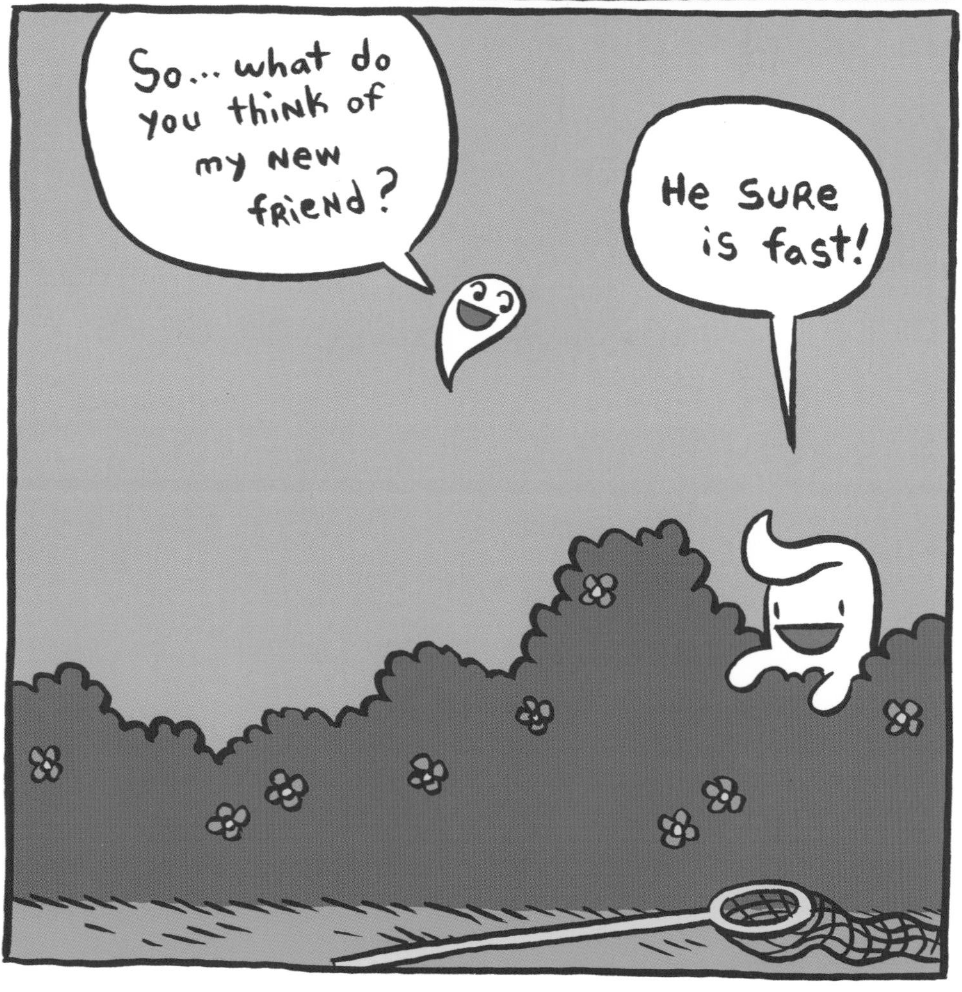
So... what do you think of my new friend?
He sure is fast!

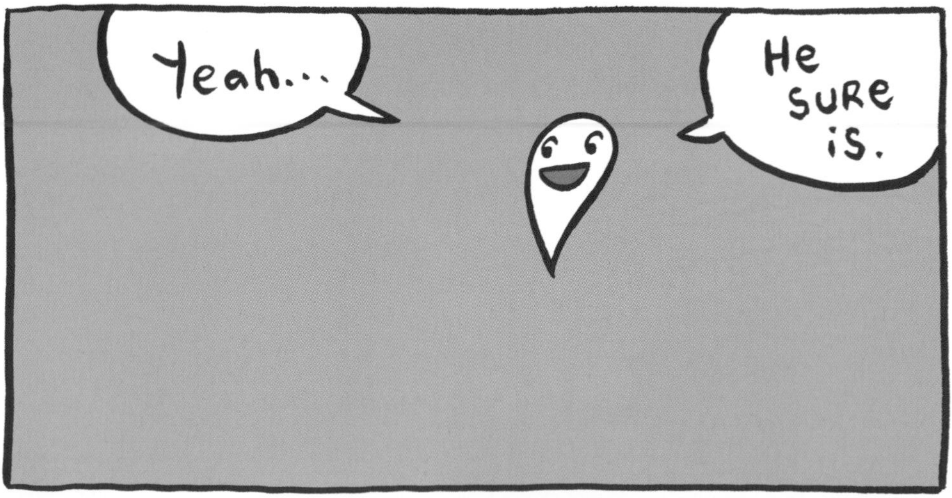
Yeah...
He sure is.

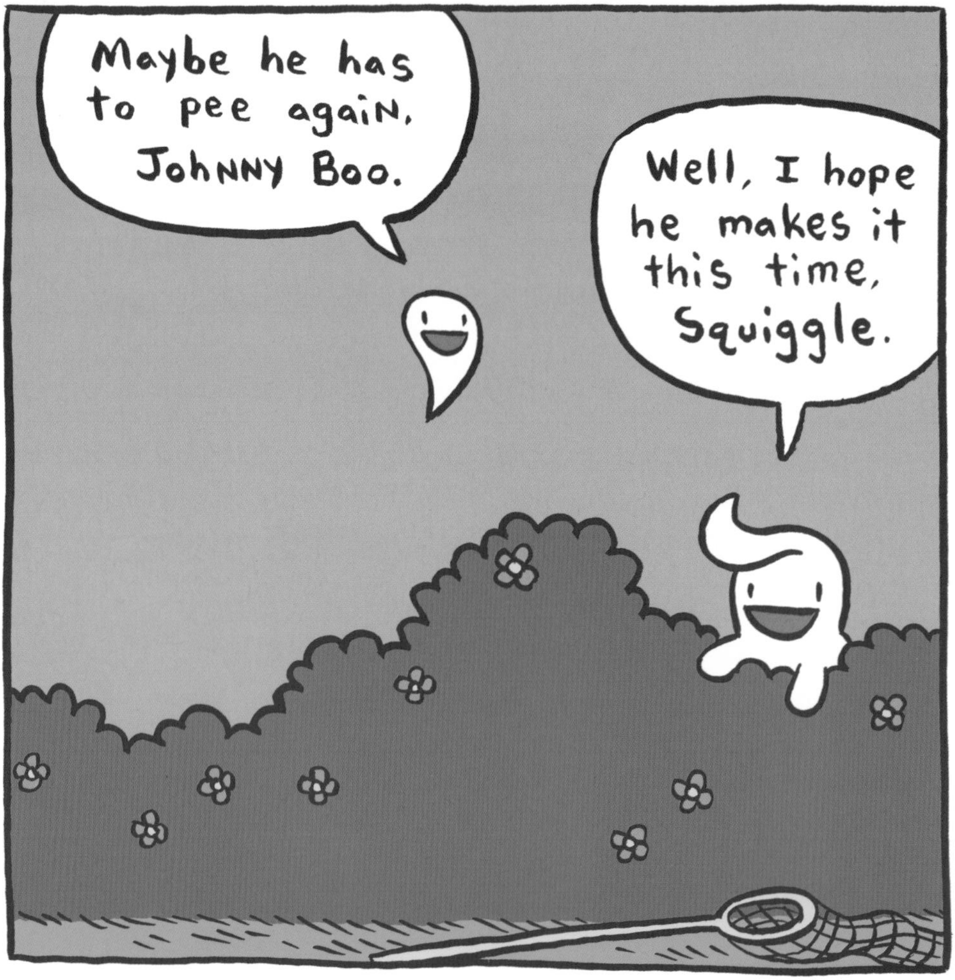
Maybe he has to pee again, Johnny Boo.
Well, I hope he makes it this time, Squiggle.

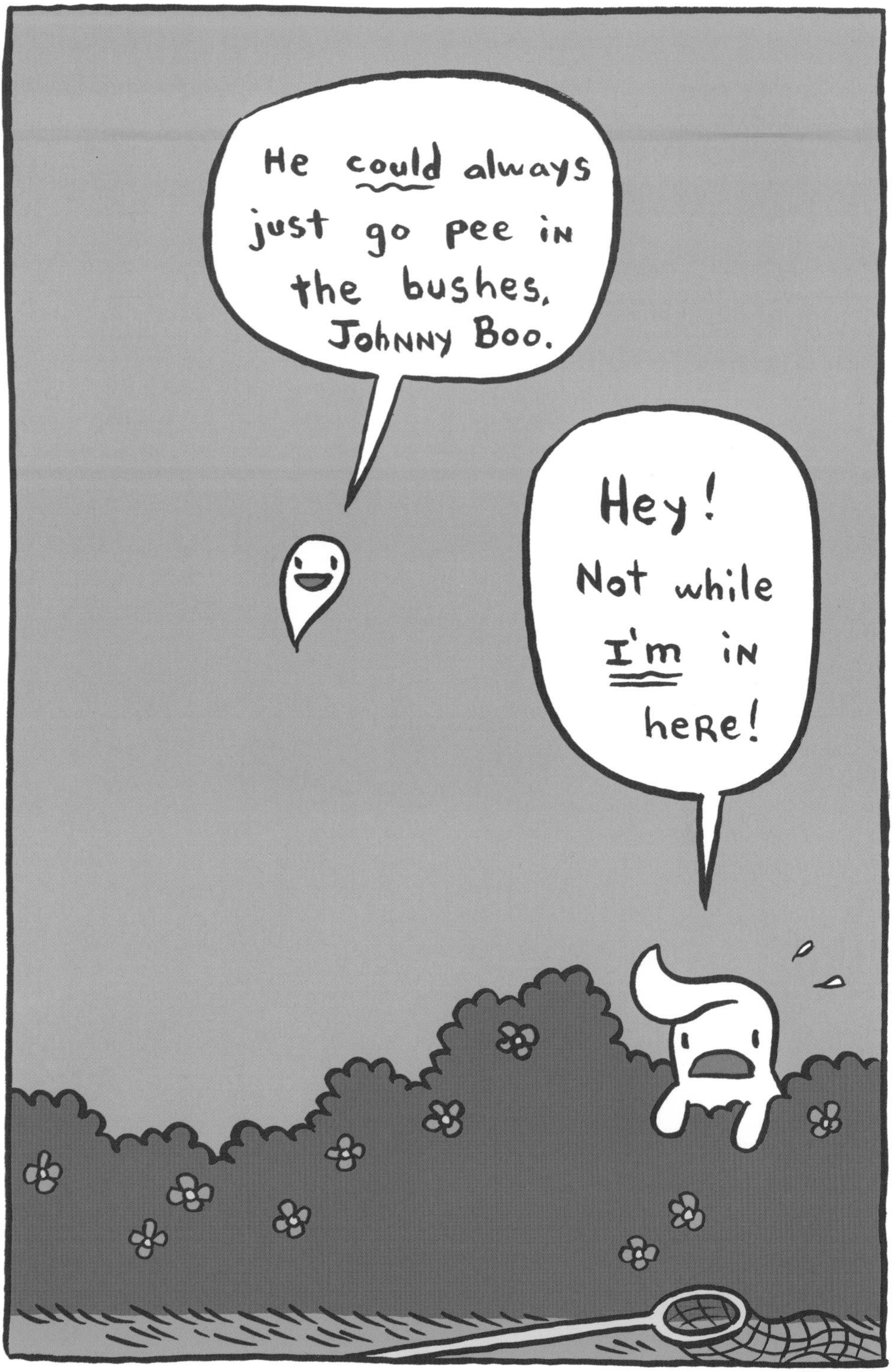
He could always just go pee in the bushes, Johnny Boo.
Hey! Not while I'm in here!

THE END

A PHOTO OF THE AUTHOR'S DRAWING HAND:

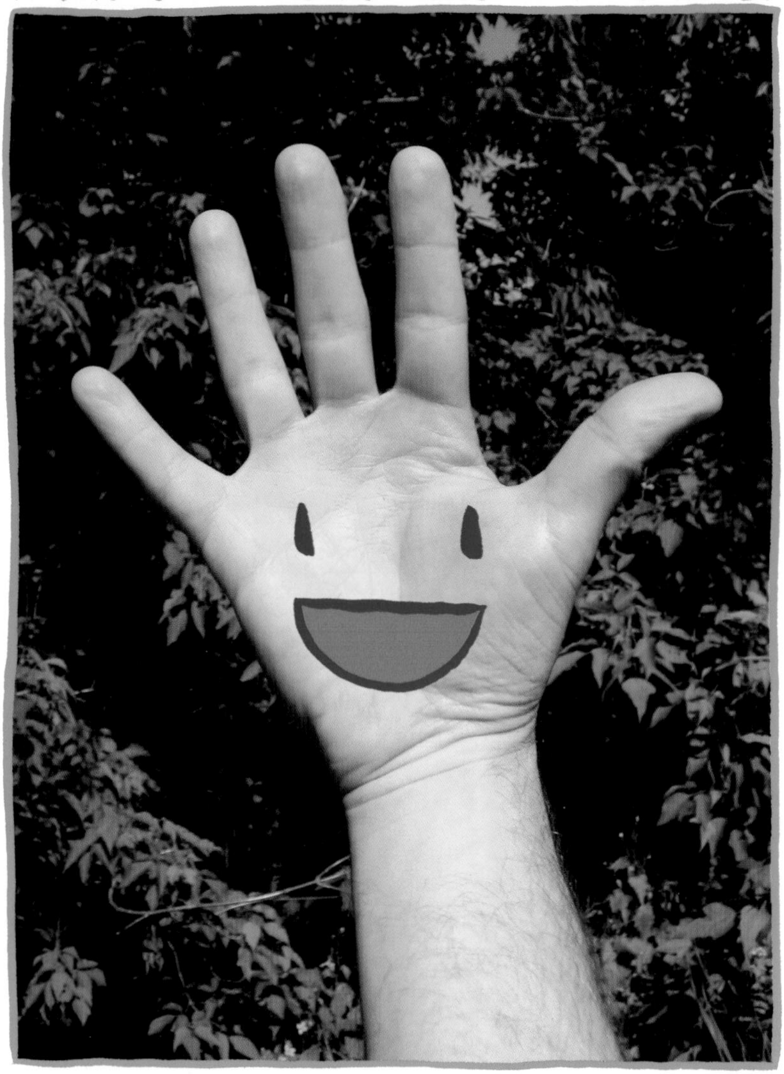